Round Corners

Mystery novel circa 1940,
New Bedford, MA - World War II era

By

Clement R Beaulieu

iUniverse LLC
Bloomington

ROUND CORNERS
MYSTERY NOVEL CIRCA 1940, NEW
BEDFORD, MA - WORLD WAR II ERA

This is a work of fiction. All of the characters, names, incidents, organizations, and dialogue in this novel are either the products of the author's imagination or are used fictitiously.

iUniverse books may be ordered through booksellers or by contacting:

iUniverse
1663 Liberty Drive
Bloomington, IN 47403
www.iuniverse.com
1-800-Authors (1-800-288-4677)

Because of the dynamic nature of the Internet, any web addresses or links contained in this book may have changed since publication and may no longer be valid. The views expressed in this work are solely those of the author and do not necessarily reflect the views of the publisher, and the publisher hereby disclaims any responsibility for them.

Any people depicted in stock imagery provided by Thinkstock are models, and such images are being used for illustrative purposes only. Certain stock imagery © Thinkstock.

ISBN: 978-1-4917-1388-4 (sc)
ISBN: 978-1-4917-1404-1 (e)

Printed in the United States of America.

iUniverse rev. date: 11/07/2013

Round Corners

To Sarah and Justin Ziobro

I'm grateful to my daughter, Sarah, for assisting me in the income tax office and her husband, Justin, for maintaining our property, which allowed me the time and leisure to write this story.

This mystery is a work of fiction. It continues a previous story and focuses on persons from New Bedford, MA. Some of the historical personages mentioned in connection with the events of the story actually existed. The time of the story is circa 1940 and the era of World War II.

The main characters of the story are fictional. Retired Nurse Lieutenant Commander, Barbara O'Neill, as well as members of my family have provided me with actual events or experiences in their lives or of their loved ones who served in the military during the war. Their sharing has assisted me in putting a touch of realism to this tale. However, any resemblance to actual persons living or dead is strictly coincidental.

A special thanks to my cousin, Richard, who provided the photograph that, was used for the front cover of the book. My daughter, Julia, has again provided an original watercolor that is used as the background of the back cover. I am grateful for the support that my wife Jo-Ann continues to bring to these projects. Joyce Poirier has continued to encourage me in the writing of *Round Corners* which is the sequel to *Bad Lucky Number*.

Round Corners

Book One

Round Corners

Book One

Chapter One

Early 1941, New Bedford, MA.:

Joao Pimentel woke up around 4 o'clock. He had not slept well. He was a mason with a local contractor. Work had been hard to come by the last few years. His boss, Domingos Medeiros, had started a project renovating an old home that had been vacant for at least two years. The structure had been built in 1828. It was a beautiful example of a Greek revival home seen on the plantations of Georgia. Six stately columns graced the entrance and provided a shaded porch facing east toward the fishing port of New Bedford. It was set back from the busy thoroughfare and was just a few blocks away from the Wamsutta Club.

Joao was grateful for this steady work. During his months of unemployment, his large Portuguese family had rallied together to provide for everyone's needs. His wife Maria, who slept near him, had prayed many rosaries during those days. Two of Joao's daughters had gotten work in the clothing mills putting in long hours working at sewing machines. They were paid by the number of items they produced during their shift. It was called piecework. When they first started both were very slow and the earnings were meager. The younger of the sisters, however, soon discovered that she had an innate talent for handling the sewing machine.

Joao had grown a fine vegetable garden on the small parcel behind their home. In the basement kitchen used for cooking, Maria and her mother Paula spent many hours making meals that provided for a family of ten. Along with the three girls, there were two young boys and Joao's sickly parents and Maria's mother. Joao's oldest son, Antone, worked as a delivery boy for a small market just a few blocks from their home in the West End of the city. He took great care of the bicycle his godfather had given him. It was equipped with a large metal basket used for deliveries that extended from the handlebars and over the front wheel. Antone was especially proud of the bright green and red tassels that flared out of his handlebar grips.

The owner of the market, Dinis Vieira, gave Antone about one dollar a week for the deliveries he made on Saturdays and after school hours, usually on Thursdays and Fridays. What the whole family appreciated most from Antone's work at the market was the cuts of meat that Mr. Vieira would offer to Antone at the close of the day on Saturday. Everyone would gather around to see Antone's prize possession. Most times it was an end piece of beef or pork and occasionally a whole fish.

Joao reached over and kissed his wife, Maria. She immediately awakened and gathered her housecoat around her as she shuffled to the bathroom before Joao. "I'll brew a pot of coffee," she said as she went to the kitchen. "How would you like your eggs this morning?" Joao answered, "A couple of nice runny ones and two thick crusts of bread."

Joao put on his blue coveralls over a heavy plaid shirt. The days were getting a little cooler, not untypical for mid-September.

When Joao entered the kitchen Maria was seated at the small kitchen table drinking a large cup of strong coffee. Joao's plate of cooked eggs and bread sat at his side of the table. Joao sat and looked to Maria, "I'm a bit nervous today. Mr. Medeiros has asked me to remove the tiles in one of the bathrooms. Last week I worked with the majority of the crew pointing and replacing exterior bricks of the huge fireplace on the south side of the house. This work in the bathroom is finer work and requires precision not to break the white

4

tiles as they are removed. Mr. Medeiros chose me specifically since he said he knew and appreciated my skills and methodic approach. He told me he wants to use these tiles in another future project. I appreciate his confidence in me and I hope I don't disappoint him."

When Joao arrived at the work site, Domingos Medeiros directed, "Joao come with me." Joao followed Mr. Medeiros to the second floor toward the rear of the building. He started telling Joao, "I inspected the bathroom last evening after work. You'll notice that the old clawfoot tub has been removed as well as the plumbing. There are a few wall tiles that are broken. However, we can use the same flat flooring tiles that were used on the raised platform to replace them or any that might get broken when they are removed." Joao appreciated that statement. It took some pressure off this delicate task that was given to him.

"Where you need to be especially careful, Joao," continued Mr. Medeiros, "is removing the curved tiles there at the corner and the carved tiles that top the five foot tile walls at the front and side of the tub. I'm not sure if we could easily find replacement tiles for those. Don't be afraid to destroy the walls above and around the tiles if it assists in removing them. The walls are made of horsehair plaster. We will eventually gut the entire bathroom and use a new Gypsum wallboard panel that is easily installed. The developer wants to provide this home with the latest fashion shower and bath that will be adjacent to the master suite."

When Mr. Medeiros left the room, Joao started to inspect the tile walls and raised flooring. He decided that he would start removing the tiles on the flooring. Some were already loose, possibly from dampness and the settling of the subfloor. Equipped with a rubber hammer and a wide chisel, Joao started to remove the floor tiles. Occasionally, some of the tiles came off in sections. Within a few hours the tiles from the raised flooring had been removed. Only two tiles had broken in two, one was on the edge of the raised platform and had shown a faint line and the other was the one where the drain had been drilled to remove the water from the tub.

Joao inspected the wall that had been drilled to supply cold and hot water to the tub. That area was also weakened by past dampness. The challenge was to remove the curved tiles on the edge and the carved tiles at the top. Joao decided to remove about two feet of the horsehair plaster that was adjacent to the tile walls. The horsehair plaster was attached to a lattice of wooden slats. Once Joao had removed the plaster and slats from the side and top of the front section, he was able to get a better view of the work area. The grout that held the edge tiles was easily chiseled away. The carved tiles at the top posed a greater challenge. The opening in the wall that Joao had made allowed him to put some pressure from the rear of the wall. This allowed a section to become loosened and pointed to areas where the grout could be chiseled away. With care Joao was able to successfully remove a large section.

As Joao was getting ready to leave the work site, Mr. Medeiros came to see what progress Joao had made on removing the white tiles. "Great job, Joao," commented Mr. Medeiros, as Joao explained his approach to removing the tiles on the walls. Mr. Medeiros said, "I'll have someone assist you tomorrow. The side panel is very large and if you can remove some of it in sections, I'm sure an extra hand would be helpful. "

Joao went home to Maria a happy man. He found Maria and her mother in the basement kitchen preparing supper. Maria was a great listener. Every day when Joao came home from work, he related the events of his day. Most times Maria didn't understand or appreciate the details of the work he had been doing but she knew that it was important for Joao to share his day with her. Also she was especially sensitive to the feelings he expressed and would offer comfort and praise. During these sessions Maria's mother just kept busy almost unaware that Joao was in the room.

Round Corners

Chapter Two

The next morning Domingos Medeiros introduced Joao to Jean Paul Lepage. "I've known Jean Paul since he was a boy. I built a milk dairy facility for his father quite a few years ago. Unfortunately, Mr. Lepage had to sell his dairy during the Depression. Jean Paul is a hard worker and I'm confident he will be of great assistance."

Most of the morning Joao and his assistant removed the plaster and lattice around the sidewall that bordered the white tiles. Joao pointed out to Jean Paul; "Do you see that rough indentation over the center of the tiles? It looks like someone repaired a rather large hole. The work is a very different quality of workmanship than the original plastering on the rest of walls and ceiling of this room."

Work on the project proceeded quite smoothly. Large sections were removed rather easily from the area that had been closest to the end of the original bathtub. When Joao started to inspect the area toward the center of that wall where he had observed the indentation and repairs, he discovered that a small wooden box had been forced behind the tiles. With Jean Paul's assistance, Joao removed it. Both men were quite curious as to the contents of the box whose lid was firmly nailed down.

Joao asked his young assistant, "Go find Mr. Medeiros. We should check with him before we open it."

Sometime later Jean Paul returned with Mr. Medeiros. Joao pointed out that a balsam wood had been used in making the box. "Do you want me to open it?" asked Joao.

"Absolutely," answered Mr. Medeiros. "I'm very curious to find out its contents. One never knows what treasures are hidden in these old houses."

Joao carefully loosened the lid from the box. Something was wrapped in a rich looking material.

"Remove it carefully," instructed Mr. Medeiros. After Joao had laid it down on a clear section of the bathroom floor, Mr. Medeiros bent down and started to unwrap the cloth from whatever it contained. Suddenly all three of the men let out a gasp of fright. It contained the skeletal remains of a tiny infant.

Mr. Medeiros quickly jumped up from his stooped position. All three looked at each other in disbelief. "Oh, Jesu!" cried Joao as he crossed himself. Jean Paul felt the blood drain from his head and thought he might faint.

Mr. Medeiros eventually breathed in deeply and instructed Jean Paul to go straight away to the police station just down Union Street. "Some terrible tragedy has occurred in this house. Ask the police chief to send someone here immediately. Joao and I will remain here and leave everything as it is now. Go quickly."

After what seemed like hours, Jean Paul entered the upstairs room followed by two men. The thin gentleman in the long trench coat introduced himself, "I'm Inspector Daniel O'Malley and this is detective William Normandin. The Police Chief has personally directed me to conduct this investigation. From the little information this young man was able to relate to the Police Chief, we are prepared to take all necessary measures to resolve this dreadful and repellent discovery."

Joao explained how they had come upon the box hidden in the wall. Mr. Medeiros stated, "I personally unwrapped what I originally thought concealed some treasures from previous occupants."

Inspector O'Malley knelt beside the remains of what was evidently once a very young infant. "The coroner's office is sending someone to examine these small bones. Dr. Kendall has recently been given assistance in his lab from the State's pathology department located at Massachusetts General Hospital. He is a recent graduate from Boston University and has been trained in the latest forensic tools available."

Not long afterwards, a young man of medium height with a dark ponytail entered the room. He was equipped with a black instrument that hung from a strap on his left shoulder. He introduced himself, "My name is David Rubin. Before I start asking questions, please stay exactly as you are. I want to take detailed photographs of the crime scene." He quickly swung the camera from his shoulder while adjusting and turning screws that expanded the lens. He moved about the room taking pictures from every angle.

"Thank you for your cooperation. You too, Inspector." O'Malley was still kneeling near the small bundle. "Who made the discovery?" continued David Rubin. Mr. Medeiros explained the sequence of events. Both Inspector O'Malley and the young assistant coroner were making entries in their notepads.

The assistant coroner continued, "Who actually touched the box in which the remains were found?" Joao explained, "I removed the box stuffed in the walls with the assistance of my helper, Jean Paul. I was the only one who touched it after that. I was the one that inspected it and removed the lid. I was the one who removed the wrapped package from the box." Mr. Medeiros interjected, "I was the one that unwrapped the small parcel and discovered the remains."

Young David Rubin looked to the Inspector, "When we are finished here, would you please escort these two men," pointing at Joao and Jean Paul, "to the police station and take their fingerprints?" O'Malley nodded that he would do so. David Rubin continued, "I will attempt to take fingerprints from the box to see if it reveals prints other than these two men."

David Rubin had entered the room with a light pair of what seemed rubber gloves. He handed a similar pair of gloves to Detective Normandin. With Detective Bill Normandin's assistance, David Rubin placed the box, cloth parcel and some of the plaster wall and tiles on a slab and carefully covered it with a thick white cloth for transport. "Inspector," continued the assistant coroner, "please secure this room. I will want to return to it for further examination." He turned to Mr. Medeiros and said, "Avoid working in direct proximity to this room either above it, below it or to the sides. And if any of your men find anything that looks suspicious or out of the ordinary, please contact me immediately."

Inspector O'Malley thanked everyone for their cooperation. He instructed Detective Normandin, "Please accompany Mr. Rubin to the morgue. When you have a more detailed report, let's meet back at the station." Joao and the Inspector walked together down Union Street to the central police station. A very nervous Jean Paul followed closely behind them.

Round Corners

Chapter Three

As Jean Paul Lepage was being fingerprinted, he asked, "How is the taking of my fingerprints going to be helpful?" The policeman who was imprinting his thumb and fingers on a card explained, "Just before the turn of the century, an Englishman named Sir Francis Galton, determined that the prints from our fingers are all unique to a person. Plus, they don't even change over time. He identified five details that are common at the tips of your fingers that I am capturing by placing the tips of each of your fingers in printer's ink and spreading that fingertip on paper."

The policeman continued, "If you look closely to the tip of your forefinger that I just copied, you can see what are called ridges. Some are short. Some split up and those are called forking ridges. That one is enclosed and it is called an island. Dalton calculated that the odds of two individuals having exactly the same fingerprints were about 1 in 64 billion. England and Wales soon began to use fingerprints for criminal identification. A few years later the U. S. Army began using fingerprints for personal identification."

"Wow," said Jean Paul. "But how is that going to help?" The policeman explained, "According to what I've heard, a box was found with a small corpse in it and you and the other gentleman I just finished fingerprinting were the only ones who touched it. There is a way of lifting your fingerprints from that box. If we find fingerprints that don't match yours or the other gentleman, than we can try to find to whom they belong."

Jean Paul started to reach to his head with his blackened fingers. "Before, you touch anything," interjected the policeman, "wipe your hands with this towel." Jean Paul thanked him. He started to scratch his head with an inquisitive look on his face. "How do you find the person whose prints may be on the box?" he inquired. "There are many files of fingerprints available to the police department," explained the policeman. "We could never randomly search those files for a match. However, if we could discover the people who previously lived at the house you are working on, we would narrow down the field of our investigation. And for example, if one of the persons associated with the house was someone who served in the military, we would have a good chance of finding that file and see if the prints match."

"Oh, I see," said Jean Paul. "Wow, you mean my fingerprints belong only to me. There is no one else in the world who has or even ever had a fingerprint exactly like mine?" "That's right." "And my fingerprints never change even when I'm old and gray?" "Right, again."

"You're a curious young fellow, aren't you," commented the policeman. "You must be a good student." "Oh, I'm alright, I guess. I especially enjoy going to the library and looking through the National Geographic magazines. There are so many different places in the world and people live so differently from us. Someday I would like to travel around the world."

Jean Paul couldn't wait to share this new discovery with his brother, Pierre. He skipped down the stairs of the police station and ran up to the Avenue. He waited for the trolley that would bring him to the north end of the city. When he was younger he had traveled a few times when the trolley ran on the rails that were now being removed from the city streets. The trolleys were now equipped with large rubber tires, similar to the ones on cars and trucks. They were still powered by the wires above them but he had heard that even that was changing. The new trolleys would soon be powered with their own gasoline engine.

As he sat in the trolley, Jean Paul recalled the frightening sight that confronted him when Mr. Medeiros unwrapped the parcel. An ache clutched at his throat. A baby a few months old had recently died in the neighborhood. Jean Paul was a good friend of the dead baby's brother. Richard lived across the street and together they walked to and from St. Joseph's school. Jean Paul had keenly felt the anguish and pain of his friend, Richard. They had spent some time together under a tree in the park above the Avenue. Richard cried occasionally and Jean Paul just stayed with him. Jean Paul who always had lots to say and questions to ask, sat mostly quiet beside his friend. A few times he had reached and put an arm around his friend's shoulder.

Round Corners

Chapter Four

Detective Bill Normandin quietly observed while Doctor Kendall and David Rubin examined the small skeletal remains on the metal table. David pointed out, "First, we see clear evidence that the child at its death was less than two years old. The bones of the cranial vault have not interlocked at the sutures. The fibrous tissue membranes that have deteriorated did not have sufficient time to ossify." Doctor Kendall concurred, "It is certainly in keeping with the overall size of this skeleton."

David Rubin began examining the jaw area. He stated, "At birth we know that the mandible," and looking over his shoulder to the detective, "what we commonly call the jaw is in two separate halves. And that is what we see here. Again the two halves of the jaw are normally joined at the median plane of the symphysis by fibrous tissue. Union of the two halves is normally completed by 12 months of age. We have the skeletal remains of an infant that is less than a year old."

Doctor Kendall observed, "From my years of experience delivering babies, I am of the opinion that this child was only slightly larger than a newborn. I would tend to conclude that the child did not die at childbirth but lived for at least a few weeks. David, are there any newer forensic studies that would narrow down that first year of life?" "From my studies to date, I am not aware of any other evidence available from the study of a skeleton," answered David.

Bill inquired, "Can you determine the sex of the child who was placed behind the walls of that building?" David pointed to the pelvic area of the small skeletal remains; "Present forensic science can identify differences between adult male and female pelves. It is apparent in the overall size, proportions and morphology. However, there is an overlap in the male and female ranges of variation. When sex determination is based entirely on the pelvis, the degree of accuracy is at best 85 percent and that applies only to adults. In these skeletal remains the large irregularly shaped bone called the innominate is still separated into three parts. The union of these bones is normally completed by 23 years of age. A quick answer to your question is unfortunately, no."

"Can it be determined how long this child has been dead?" asked Bill. "Professionally, I am certain that the child's initial resting place was not behind the wall of the house. The remains were moved there as many as two years after his or her death. The small body has become almost completely skeletalized.

Not only are the skin and soft tissues not present, but also missing are the cartilage and ligaments that connect the bones together. Also the cloth in which the bones were wrapped shows almost no sign of decomposition," answered David.

Dr. Kendall observed, "These tiny remains were decomposed prior to being stored in the wall. Someone wrapped these bones very carefully and probably with tenderness. The bones were carefully gathered and placed in its normal skeletal form and not just indiscriminately on this fine piece of silken cloth." Addressing David Rubin, Dr. Kendall asked, "Is there any evidence as to where the skeleton had been prior to it being hidden behind the wall of that bathroom?"

"We will have to do a more extensive examination," answered David. "If we can detect that the remains had been buried, we may be able to find a trace of the soil's composition and find a uniqueness that would point to a certain location. That is probably a very long shot. However, if we detect soil and clear indications that these remains were buried, than studies have shown that it will take between 1 and

2 years to become skeletalized. If the body was left on the surface of the ground, insect activity would begin immediately and the remains would be in this condition within 8 months."

"Is there anything else you can tell us that will help us in this investigation?" asked Bill. "A quick examination of the skull and other bones do not indicate any blunt trauma. Upon further investigation we may discover the presence of a foreign substance that points to poisoning. A study of the bones could provide clues like malnutrition. However, the cause of death may have been very natural. We would need to bring these precious remains to the lab in Boston where there are tools and equipment that have been developed to ascertain such type of information."

"There are other studies that may assist the investigation," continued David. "We will examine the cloth that wrapped these bones and the box in which they were contained. A study of the bathroom and its walls could also provide some helpful clues."

"Thank you for your observations and conclusions so far," commented Bill. "I will bring this information to the Inspector. If and when your forensic studies reveal additional clues as to the death of this child, please contact us."

Round Corners

Chapter Five

Jean Paul was surprised to meet his brother Claude at the entrance of Ben Labonte's pharmacy. "What are you doing here?" asked Jean Paul. "One of my co-workers gave me a ride home from Portsmouth," answered Claude. "We just finished constructing another version of a Quonset Hut. The engineers are going to study it over the weekend for structural strength and flexibility in dissembling and reconstructing it in the field. The Navy is looking to produce many of these to be sent overseas. We were given the weekend off. We need to report back early Monday."

"Let me buy you a frappe," suggested Claude. "I just got paid and I feel flush at the moment. When we get home I'll be giving most of my earnings to help with family expenses. How are you doing, little brother?"

"A few weeks ago I started to work for Mr. Medeiros, the contractor," answered Jean Paul. "He told me that he built Pa's milk dairy in Acushnet. I'm just a helper but learning a lot. Today, I received the scare of my life."

While sitting together at the stainless steel counter, Jean Paul related the events that had occurred earlier. "I don't know if I want to fall asleep tonight," stated Jean Paul. "I'm afraid I'll have nightmares."

Sarah Labonte approached the counter and expressed great happiness in seeing the two young men. Through Al Lepage, the bread and donut man, Sarah and her husband Ben had gotten to know the many Lepages that lived down the street from the drug store. "You boys have grown so much," she stated excitedly. She was pleased to know that both were working.

Claude stated, "I haven't said this to any of the family yet," as he looked at his brother, "but I'm considering enlisting in the Navy. There is word out there that a new Naval Construction Battalion is being organized. A few years ago the Navy became convinced that war is coming. Recently they started a program building bases on some of the very distant islands in the Pacific using civilian contractors."

As people in the drug store heard Claude talking of war, they became quiet and listened intently, trying to grasp every word. One of the patrons even went to get Ben who was in the back room putting together medicines.

Claude hadn't anticipated this curiosity and he didn't want to create any alarm in anyone. At the base where he worked, such conversations were so common that it seemed part of life. Considering his words more carefully Claude continued, "I've been working on the development of a light prefab structure similar to one used by the British in World War I. The new design is in its final stages and is being called a Quonset Hut since prototypes are being designed and built at Quonset Point in Rhode Island. The hut is mainly made of curved corrugated steel sheets attached with nuts and bolts. We've improved on the original British hut by using a pressed wood, Masonite, on the interior walls, which covers insulation. A one-inch tongue-in-groove plywood floor is placed on a metal framework."

"The plan is to send these lightweight corrugated steel sheets and other parts of the structure to distant places and that a crew of 6 to 8 men would erect the hut in a day," continued Claude. "That's why I'm planning to join that group which some are suggesting that they be called Seabees."

On their way to the family three-decker down the street from the pharmacy, Jean Paul asked, "What do you think Ma will say about your plan to join the Navy?"

"I hope to convince her and Pa that this is similar to what I'm doing now but only not close to home," answered Claude.

"You'd keep in touch with us, won't you?" asked Jean Paul. "No one in the family has ever gone far away."

"Of, course, I'll keep in touch," said Claude as he rubbed his hand on the head of his young brother.

Round Corners

Book Two

Round Corners

Book Two

Chapter Six

Searching for clues:

Detective Normandin brought Inspector O'Malley up do date on the forensic evidence that Doctor Kendall and his new assistant had concluded so far in the investigation of the small skeletal remains.

"It's unbelievable how much information they were able to get from their brief examination," exclaimed Bill Normandin. "David wants to bring the remains to the forensic lab in Boston. There are special investigative tools and equipment there that could assist in determining the time of death and the original place of burial. I'm in awe of this type of study. I appreciate your assistance in encouraging me to enter the police academy. I wouldn't be a detective today if you hadn't brought me on your team so many years ago for the Gabriel Beaumont homicide. You've assisted in opening my eyes and imagination to a whole new world."

"Would you be interested in pursuing this type of investigation?" asked Inspector O'Malley. "What I'm thinking, is asking Chief Downey to let you go with David Rubin to Boston so you might observe the latest forensic methods that are being developed."

"Oh, I would be more than interested. I think the more we know about the advances in the field of forensics, the more it will assist us on the initial scene of a crime. It would caution us to be careful in preserving the integrity of the site," answered Bill Normandin. He was suddenly aware that he was using terms he had heard from David Rubin.

"In the meantime, I want you to research the history of the house on County Street," continued O'Malley. "Knowledge of the prior occupants might help in finding whoever hid the remains behind those walls. Also follow up with the contractor, Mr. Medeiros, and his mason, Joao Pimentel. According to my notes, the mason stated that he had noticed that the wall had been previously repaired. See if he can estimate from his expertise a proximate time when this work was done. Let's get together tomorrow around four."

Round Corners

Chapter Seven

Detective Bill Normandin arrived at the central police station a little after four. Inspector O'Malley was quick to quiz his new detective. "What have you discovered, Bill?"

Bill removed his notepad from the inner pocket of his gray suit coat. This was a far cry from his earlier days of writing notes on pieces of assorted papers. Then of course he was a street patrolman. Classes in criminal justice and at the police academy had prepared him for these assignments.

"The house where the skeletal remains were found," started Bill, "is one of the many homes in a neighborhood that go back to the whaling era. A well-preserved house on the same side of County Street is the Horatio Hathaway House. Horatio Hathaway founded the Hathaway Manufacturing Company in 1888 as a cotton mill. Mr. Hathaway had been a China trader who profited from his once successful whaling business in the Pacific Ocean. He knew from his travel and connections in the whaling industry that New Bedford was expanding rapidly in the production of fine cotton goods."

"There is a well-documented history of the Hathaway House," continued Bill. "That house was built in 1828. County registry records for the house we are investigating are less conclusive. There is a statement in the records that point to a builder of at least three whaling ships. These ships were built in neighboring Mattapoisett. When he decided to captain one of the ships that he had built, Captain Anthony Spooner moved his family into the New Bedford house. It was equipped with a small viewing area above the house now referred to as a widow's walk. It provided a great view of the harbor and its entrance through Buzzards Bay."

"The assistant at the Bristol County Registrar's office was quite positive that even though the house over the years had quite a few owners on the deed, all were related to or descendants of Anthony Spooner," stated Bill Normandin.

Inspector O'Malley asked, "Were you able to discover the last occupants of the house?"

"The house was sold by Abigail Spooner Weigand," answered Bill. "Abigail had married an Ethan Weigand of New York City some years previously. The title of the house, however, was only in her maiden name. Mrs. Clara Bonworth at the Registry thought that there might have been a stipulation in Captain Spooner's last will and testament that only a descendant could inherit the building. I suspect that further investigation will show that the present owner, Charles Gurney, who engaged Mr. Medeiros to upgrade and renovate this old house, is also a distant relative."

"What did you learn about Mrs. Abigail Spooner Weigand?" asked O'Malley. The inspector was looking at his notes where he had recorded names and other details that Bill Normandin had related to him.

"I questioned a few of the neighbors," answered Bill. "Most were tight lipped and reluctant to provide any information even when I showed them my official detective badge. This is so different from my old neighborhood where sharing gossip or facts flowed freely. However, one neighbor did tell me that Abigail moved into the house from Dartmouth soon after she married Mr. Weigand. The marriage lasted less than ten years."

"Did the Weigand's have any children?" inquired O'Malley. Bill Normandin could sense that the Inspector was trying to pull together information that would be helpful in solving the mystery of the dead child. He was professionally controlling his curiosity but trying not to leave any tiny bit of information escape them.

"The neighbor on the north side of the house volunteered that information," answered Bill. "My questions seemed to loosen her tongue and she seemed anxious to learn the nature of my investigation. I didn't share our discovery. She told me that she had only observed one child over the years. Abigail had been very private and almost a recluse in her later years."

Bill continued, "The child she had seen was a sickly looking young boy who stayed mostly to himself. Except for the small staff who helped with household duties and in his care, she had never seen him with any other children. She thought that his name was Mortimer. The housemaid had a daughter a few years older than the boy. From her perch at the second floor window, the neighbor had heard her call out to him but he always seemed to ignore her."

"Did you get any information as to the proximate age of this young man?" asked O'Malley.

"I was able to put this together from information provided by the neighbors," answered Bill. "Abigail and her husband David moved into the house about thirty years ago. They remembered a great festivity. It was the last time the neighbors had been invited to the Weigand residence. After a few years David Weigand seemed to spend less and less time at home. At first they didn't think it strange as they had learned that he owned and managed a factory in the garment section of New York City. He had proudly told those who had attended that original party that his company provided exquisite dresses to Macy's Department store. Both neighbors thought the boy, Mortimer, was about five years old at the time of the divorce."

Round Corners

Chapter Eight

Inspector O'Malley had been standing behind his desk during the entire time that Detective Normandin answered his questions. Again he was amazed and reassured that his new detective had been thorough and insightful.

O'Malley sat down in his chair. "Bill, please have a seat. I'm afraid I was putting you through quite the inquisition. This strange death of a little child has unnerved me. My two girls are now teenagers but I still feel very protective of them and other children. Let's continue. I promise to take a few deep breaths every once in a while. Were you able to learn the whereabouts of Abigail? Is she even still alive?"

"Mrs. Abigail Spooner Weigand is quite ill," answered Bill. "Around the time of the sale of the County Street house, she moved with her attendant into the Fairhaven Residence in our neighboring town across the river. This residence provides medical support to about ten women. A personal nurse or former housekeeper accompanies most women."

"Do you know what happened to her son, Mortimer?" asked O'Malley. "One of the neighbors felt quite confident that he went off to a boarding school in New Hampshire," answered Bill. "Abigail, I was told, spent most of her summer months in upstate New York. Being off to a boarding school during the winter months and assuming he joined his mother in upstate New York in the summer, Mortimer was only infrequently seen at his home in New Bedford. He should be about twenty years old, now. I'm sure there is a lot more we can uncover about the Weigands and their son, Mortimer."

O'Malley continued his questioning, "Were you able to get together with Mr. Medeiros, the contractor, and his mason?"

"No," answered Bill Normandin. "My somewhat fruitful interviews with the Weigand neighbors on County Street and the two times I visited the Registry of Deeds just about filled my day."

"Let's plan some strategy," stated the Inspector. "Chief Downey has agreed to your travelling with David Rubin to Boston. Do you know when he plans to go to the lab?" asked O'Malley.

"He is planning to bring the remains to the forensic lab next Wednesday, September 20th. One of his professors who is also a pathologist at the State lab has agreed to meet with David and assist in the examination of the child's skeletal remains. He has invited me to have supper with his family before heading back to New Bedford," answered Bill.

"This is how we will proceed," stated O'Malley. "Let's take the weekend to be with our families. On Monday focus on the house on County Street. See if the contractor and his mason can approximate a time when the remains were stored behind the bathroom wall. In the meantime, I will interview Mrs. Weigand. Along with the information she might provide, I will try to learn the names of the members of Abigail's household staff during her years on County Street. They could provide more first hand information. Let's meet at four on Monday."

Round Corners

Chapter Nine

Inspector Daniel O'Malley entered the Fairhaven Residence at exactly ten o'clock. His punctuality was well known. It was admired and appreciated by some, while others found it aggravating. There was little O'Malley could do, with what some called an obsession. It was the only way he knew how to work. He could however adapt to other people's tardiness without complaint or evident agitation. O'Malley exhibited great patience and appreciation of others. Those who worked most regularly with him eventually almost always fell into his rhythm.

O'Malley had called in advance so that he was expected at the residence. The receptionist directed him to an apartment at the rear of the building. A gray haired lady welcomed him and introduced herself as Mrs. Moriarity. O'Malley easily detected the Irish accent. "Could you be originally from County Galway?" asked O'Malley. Mrs. Moriarity blushed in ascent and added, "I'm assuming you're of Irish descent." "Oh, sure," answered O'Malley adding a little Irish accent of his own. He was having a little good humor with his new acquaintance. It often helped to smooth the way with the questioning that would come later. "I was born in the Irish section of Dorchester. My mother came from Sligo and my father fared from Kerry," answered the Inspector.

Mrs. Moriarity took the Inspector's dark blue fedora and placed it on a table in the tiny foyer of the apartment. "I've told Mrs. Spooner that you were coming. She is expecting you. Her memory is failing so we may have to assist her in remembering what I told her earlier this morning."

O'Malley noticed that Mrs. Moriarity had referred to her employer by her maiden name. "It is my understanding that your lady was originally married to a Ethan Weigand. Did she revert to her maiden name after their divorce?" inquired O'Malley. Mrs. Moriarity seemed impressed and raised an eyebrow to express herself. "Even before the divorce was final," answered Mrs. Moriarity, "she had reverted to her maiden name. I don't think it was ever done officially."

Mrs. Abigail Spooner was seated facing a small courtyard of the residence. The room was filled with a warm morning sun. She had a colorful shawl spread across her knees. "It's a pleasure to meet you, Mrs. Spooner," said the Inspector. When Mrs. Spooner extended her hand in greeting, O'Malley grasps it gently having anticipated an elderly and weak woman. He was not surprised by the limp handshake he received in return. It matched the blanched pallor of her skin.

"My name is Daniel O'Malley. I'm an inspector for the New Bedford police department," O'Malley said as he introduced himself. "Mrs. Moriarity has probably already informed you that we are investigating a strange incident at your former home on County Street."

"Oh, yes," agreed Mrs. Spooner. "It was such a beautiful old home filled with many happy memories of my youth when I visited my Aunt Beatrice for the holidays. The years I lived there after I married Mr. Weigand, however, were quite different. After the birth of our son, Mortimer, who was quite sickly and required much of my attention, Mr. Weigand seemed constantly aggravated with me and he constantly expressed his disappointment in our young son. My heart ached to see young Mortimer receiving such constant expressions of rejection."

Mrs. Moriarity had pulled forward a chair across from Mrs. Spooner so that the Inspector could continue this conversation while being seated. Mrs. Moriarity was surprised at how quickly her lady had entered into this exchange. She was animated and alert stating quite precisely her recollections. It seemed that she had awaited such an opportunity for a long time.

"How is your son now?" inquired the Inspector. "Mortimer has grown into a healthy and fine young man," answered Mrs. Spooner. "During his childhood, Mortimer was withdrawn and sad with bouts of anger. Not only did he have to contend with the constant badgering of his father for not meeting his expectations but he also had to outgrow some infantile ailments that prevented him from many playful activities."

"When he was nine I registered Mortimer into a private boarding school in New Hampshire," continued Mrs. Spooner. "The reports from the headmaster indicated that his first year at the school was very difficult for him. Academically it was a total failure. Subjects, like mathematics and history, that Mortimer had originally expressed some interest with his tutors at home did not fare well either. I was told he befriended a young man from Long Island, New York. This young man was seemingly incorrigible. He was dismissed from the school after the first semester."

Inspector O'Malley sat quietly trying to capture all the information and nuances that just flowed from Mrs. Spooner. He didn't take out his faithful note pad. He did not want to distract her concentration. Nor did he ask the usual questions that assisted the person he was questioning to focus on the important issues of the investigation. Mrs. Spooner was doing just fine.

After a brief moment used to capture her breath, Mrs. Spooner continued, "I'm ashamed to say that my Mortimer engaged in breathing in the glue used in making model airplanes during that first semester. The young man from Long Island had introduced my Mortimer to this vile and dangerous habit. I am told that anyone who persists in this act can do serious injury to their brain."

Round Corners

Chapter Ten

Mrs. Moriarity brought in some iced tea. Inspector O'Malley followed the cues he observed and placed the linen napkin on his lap. He held the cool glass in his hands and occasionally wiped the bottom of the glass on his napkin to capture the beads of water that adhered to it.

Mrs. Spooner looked keenly into the inspector's eyes. "Fortunately, after that horrendous first year in New Hampshire, my Mortimer began to change and mature. My divorce from his father had been finalized so that he was no longer exposed to his father's ever less frequent visits to our home. I believe my decision to bring Mortimer with me to spend part of the summer at the Village of Balston Spa in upstate New York was pivotal in the change we all observed in my Mortimer," stated Mrs. Spooner as she looked to Mrs. Moriarity for confirmation. Mrs. Moriarity who sat a little to the side enjoying her glass of tea nodded in agreement.

"We stayed at the Brookside that summer," continued Mrs. Spooner. "My Mortimer seemed to enjoy the cool freshness of being in the country. He began to explore the creek at the end of the village. He marveled at the sweet aroma of chocolate that blew through town from a nearby factory. He tolerated going to the spa with me. He later told me that he couldn't stand the acrid smell of the waters that we bathed in for an hour. He was usually out of the bath and showered after fifteen minutes and would be waiting for me on the veranda."

"As for myself, I couldn't get enough of these healing baths. And it was also common for some of us to gather around the fountains, sitting with our open parasols chatting with other summer visitors and drinking a small amount of the water from the springs. I must now admit, it was not a pleasant taste but I am convinced of its healing qualities. When we returned to our home in New Bedford, it was standard procedure that Mr. Bloom needed to pack our car ... so that we had room for at least two, preferably three, large containers of the spring water. I would add a cupful to my weekly bath and drank a small amount each morning. The challenge was to stretch out our supply so that it lasted until we returned the following summer. Somehow we always seemed to manage to stretch it out." Looking at Mrs. Moriarity, "I have suspected for many years now that the supply of these spring waters were added to from our local drinking water supply. The color and taste of the water at the beginning of spring were always much lighter." Mrs. Moriarity just smiled.

Inspector O'Malley had not informed these women seated with him about the nature of the discovery in the Spooner homestead. Now that Mrs. Spooner had casually mentioned her weekly baths, he was tempted to share this information. However, he decided otherwise. There was no need to alarm them unnecessarily. The story hadn't yet hit the local paper. And he was waiting to see if Detective Bill Normandin's investigation, with the assistance of the mason, might indicate that the remains had been placed behind the bathroom wall after Mrs. Spooner had vacated the house.

"Where is your son, Mortimer?" inquired O'Malley. "I am so happy to tell you that he is a cadet at the naval academy. As I mentioned my Mortimer went through a significant transformation after our summer in Saratoga County, New York. He began to excel in his studies and for the first time joined competitive sports at the school. Because of this change I engaged Mr. Anthony Willard, president of the Whaling City National Bank and manager of my family trust, to purchase a residence for us in Saratoga Springs."

"The summers that followed," continued Mrs. Spooner, "were filled with joy. Mrs. Moriarity and her young daughter, Maureen, would join us. Mr. Bloom, our chauffeur, introduced our youngsters to the horses and their care at the racetrack. My Mortimer and Maureen would spend many hard working hours volunteering around the stables, grooming and walking horses, cleaning the stables and polishing the tack. They would return to the house brown from the sun and dirt but all smiles." Mrs. Moriarity interjected her first comment; "It was a happy time."

Inspector O'Malley took this opportunity to inquire, "May I ask, where is Mrs. Moriarity's daughter, Maureen, now?" Mrs. Spooner glanced at her side and with a graceful bow indicated that Mrs. Moriarity could answer. "Maureen is married and lives in Maryland."

"How old is your daughter?" asked O'Malley. "She just turned twenty-four a few weeks ago. Her birthday is August twenty-ninth."

Inspector O'Malley thanked Mrs. Spooner for her graciousness in accepting his request to visit with her. "Our conversation has assisted me in putting our investigation of your former residence into a real life context," stated O'Malley. After Mrs. Moriarity took his empty glass, O'Malley bid these two women farewell. There were many other questions he wanted to ask but he hoped to preserve this encounter as a conversation and not an investigation. Plus many of answers of these questions could easily come from other sources.

Just before going into the small entryway of the apartment, O'Malley turned and asked a final question, "Do you know where I may find Mr. Bloom who once worked for you?" Mrs. Spooner glanced over her shoulder. She was still facing the small courtyard of the residence. "He is in the employ of Mr. and Mrs. Wilfred Portnoy. They reside in the city."

Round Corners

Chapter Eleven

A little after four o'clock on Monday Detective Bill Normandin was seated in Inspector O'Malley's office sharing the results of his investigation of the house on County Street. "Mr. Medeiros, the contractor who is renovating the house, agreed to meet with me earlier this morning," started Bill. "He had brought Joao Pimentel, the mason, along with him."

"Both agreed that the person who placed the wooden box holding the skeletal remains behind the wall must have been an excellent carpenter," continued Bill. "The box was shaped and sized to fit perfectly into the exterior wall of the bathroom. This is a very old dwelling. He must have studied the studding of this outer wall by looking at the visible construction above this top room in the house. The attic would have provided a view of the wall and its construction. Based on those dimensions, the carpenter had designed and constructed a box that would easily slip behind the tiles around the bathtub."

"However, Mr. Pimentel was quick to state that the person who broke into the wall and sealed it back up was not a professional mason or plasterer," chuckled the detective. "He called it a terrible example of workmanship."

"Was he able to determine how long ago this happened?" asked Inspector O'Malley.

"He is convinced that it wasn't recent," answered Bill. "He ventured an opinion that the state of the plaster showed that it probably exceeded two to three years."

"That's a very important time frame," commented O'Malley. "It means the box was not placed in the wall after the Spooner family and their help vacated the premises. It happened while they were in residence."

"Someone who lived there during that time needs to know something or at least observed something," agreed Bill Normandin. "In your interview with Mrs. Spooner were you able to get any such type of information," questioned Bill.

O'Malley smiled to himself. His new detective was taking the initiative to question the Inspector - quite a role reversal. He accepted this calmly, knowing and appreciating that his new recruit was quick and very inquisitive and still needed to learn proper protocol. However, O'Malley had no desire to suppress this native talent he found so refreshing in his detective.

O'Malley answered, "Both Mrs. Spooner and her staff person, Mrs. Moriarity, shared quite openly. I had not shared with them the discovery of the skeletal remains. I did not want them to become defensive and secretive. Neither expressed any reluctance to give me a brief history of the family life and household. It took me a good hour to write down these notes in my files," pointing to the papers on his desk. "All they knew is that I was investigating an event that had come to our attention after their departure. They never inquired about the nature of the event. It didn't seem to capture their curiosity. It seems to me that if either knew that an infant's skeletal remains were behind the bathroom wall, they would have been extremely guarded."

"I agree," commented Bill Normandin. "You would have easily observed signs of nervousness and maybe even fear."

"What I discovered," continued O'Malley, "is that three other persons were in residence during those latter days in the County Street home. There was a Mr. Bloom who acted as chauffeur and general assistant around the house. He is presently working for a Portnoy family. Mrs. Spooner has a son Mortimer who is presently attending the naval academy. He had a very difficult start in his youth and his difficulties seemed to center on his father, Mr. Weigand. He and Mrs. Spooner have been divorced for quite a few years now. The other person of the household was the young daughter of Mrs. Moriarity. Her name is Maureen. She is a few years older than Mortimer. She is now married and lives in Maryland."

"We have uncovered some interesting elements in our investigation," stated O'Malley. "Yet nothing so far solves the mysterious discovery that was made in the house in question. My immediate plan is to interview Mr. Bloom, Mrs. Spooner's previous chauffeur, as early as tomorrow. When are you leaving for the laboratory in Boston?" asked the Inspector.

"Rubin is picking me up at my home at five Wednesday morning," answered Bill Normandin. "He has made arrangements for one of the coroners at the hospital who was also one of his professors to meet with us early in the morning. Barring any emergencies he hopes to put in a few hours examining and testing the skeletal remains of the child."

Detective Normandin continued, "Rubin is planning to make another visit to the Weigand residence on County Street. I was planning to join him."

"O.K.," said O'Malley. "Let's meet again tomorrow afternoon. I've spoken with the Chief and he is preparing to meet with the reporter from the Standard Times before the end of the week. He thinks it is time that we break the story to the news media. After the report of your visit to Boston, I plan to bring him up to date as to the latest results of our investigation."

O'Malley looked out his office window. There was a heavy, cold rain coming down. "Be careful on your travels," he advised Bill. "There's a nor'easter predicted for the weekend and the city of Boston often gets hit much harder than our part of the coast."

Round Corners

Chapter Twelve

On Wednesday morning Detective William Normandin was waiting on the front porch of the three-decker in the north end of the city. He still lived there with his folks and a younger sister. A steady cold rain was coming down when he saw the lights of a vehicle slowly coming up the street. It was the unmarked small white van used by the coroner's office.

After a brief greeting, David Rubin pointed to the wiper blades, "You'll soon notice that the wiper on the driver's side is not clearing away the rain very well. The one on your side seems to be working much better. I'm going to expect you to be more than a passenger and to be a second set of eyes or co-pilot."

Dawn was beginning to be evident behind the dark rainy skies as the white van left the outskirts of the city. Bill kept a keen eye on the road and occasionally pointed and alerted David to something ahead. Traffic was quite heavy even for so early in the morning, so they made slow yet steady progress.

David Rubin broke the ice and inquired, "How long have you lived in New Bedford?"

"All my life," answered Bill. "I was born and brought up in that house on Princeton Street. It's an almost exclusive French Canadian neighborhood. We all go to the same church, St. Joseph's, and its grammar school. Many families still only speak French in their homes. Our church services are conducted in French except for the Latin prayers used by the priest and answered by the altar boys. Most of the nuns who teach in the school come from Canada and many do not speak English well."

"When I first became a cop, I was a patrolman in this area. My life didn't change too much from what I had always experienced until I was drawn into providing assistance in a murder investigation," continued Bill. "My contacts in the downtown police station opened my eyes to a bigger and much more varied world. I'm still a very local boy. This is only my second trip to Boston."

"That's very interesting," said David. "I guess my very early years in Bensonhurst, NY were similar to your experience. It was an almost exclusive Jewish neighborhood. However, we left there when I was nine and moved to Boston. Our new neighborhood is a mixed bag, consisting mostly of Jews, Italians and Greeks. My years in school, especially high school and college, brought me into contact with even greater varieties of cultures and people of different economic status."

"I get the impression that you were just recently made a detective," inquired David Rubin. "Am I right?"

"It's been less than a year," answered Bill. "I had been a foot patrolman for a few years and just loved my job. I knew most of the people quite well or at least a relative if I needed to intervene in a family or neighborhood dispute. Most times I could diffuse an incident before it became a police matter."

"However, that murder case that I was asked to provide assistance changed all that," continued Bill. "It's something how the discovery of a body lying in the river behind one of the mills in my neighborhood has changed my life. Inspector Daniel O'Malley recognized some innate talent in me. He cultivated and guided my investigative abilities that helped me bring closure to that case. After that he encouraged me to take the courses and training to become a detective."

Round Corners

Chapter Thirteen

David Rubin and Bill Normandin arrived in the parking lot of Massachusetts General Hospital just before eight o'clock. David presented the white container that held evidence from the County Street house to Bill to carry. "Follow me," he stated. "We'll enter the hospital through the emergency area of the hospital. The outside doorway leading directly to the pathology laboratory is kept locked until nine o'clock. Someone in the emergency area will recognize me from my year of residency at the hospital and will allow us to proceed to the lab."

The forensic lab was empty and dark. When David threw on the light switches, the room brightened. Bill felt a cold chill in the room. It had been hot and humid on their ride into the city and the light showers that continued had dampened his shirt. David also felt a certain anxiety in being in a room lined with refrigerated slabs holding human remains.

David directed Bill to place the white container on a shiny metal table. "Before we remove our specimens, please put on this pair of gloves," requested David. "We don't want to contaminate our evidence. Doctor Malcolm who organized the residency training program in pathology should be joining us soon."

A few minutes later a tall man in a three piece suit entered the laboratory. His dark, smoothed down hair was parted in the middle. A gold chain could be seen crossing the front of his vest as he removed his jacket and put it on a hanger. He removed a white lab coat from a closet and placed his suit jacket inside. Before fastening the many buttons on his lab coat, the doctor removed the gold watch from his vest pocket and said, "Just eight o'clock. Let us begin."

After brief introductions, Dr. Malcolm began to examine the items on the stainless steel table. He had placed a large note pad on a small table adjacent to the examining table. Bill noticed that the first entry the doctor made was the time of day. "Mr. Rubin, may I ask you to assist me? We will examine this material that is already familiar to you. Also will the detective make entries in our notes as they are directed to him?" Both young men readily agreed. "You will act as my staff this morning."

While examining the wooden box, David Rubin explained that fingerprints had been lifted from the container. "Many sets of fingerprints were discovered on the box. Two sets matched the two persons who handled the box when it was discovered." Pointing to four areas both outside and inside of the small box, David explained, "These other sets of fingerprints are identical." Dr. Malcolm examined them under a microscope and concurred, "Their placement points to the conclusion that they are right and left hand of one person who handled the box. Also the fact that the fingerprints found inside the box match those on the outside, one may assume that they belong to the person who placed the box at the location of discovery."

Bill stated, "So if we are able to find the person who belongs to those fingerprints, we would be on our way of solving this mystery." Doctor Malcolm agreed with caution, "It would identify the person who placed the box in its hiding place but would not explain the death of this young child."

Doctor Malcolm turned his attention to examining the small bones that had been placed on the table. "There is clear evidence that the decay associated with these bones come from being buried in the ground and not from being placed behind a wall of a building," stated the doctor. "Studies at the University of Tennessee show that if buried, it will take between one and two years to become completely skeletalized. That is the condition of these bones. Skin, cartilage and ligaments have totally decayed."

"In the preparation of these skeletal remains for placement in the box, there is also evidence that the bones were brushed, wiped and cleaned," stated the doctor. "However, if we look closely we find some dirt present in some obstructed areas like the cranium. The amount is very little but we should be in a position to determine the inorganic minerals and metals that are present in the sample."

David Rubin interjected, "That was the main reason why I brought these skeletal remains to the Massachusetts General laboratory. We have equipment here that is capable of analyzing the material and could provide clues as to where these bones were initially buried."

"That is possible," said the doctor. "Sometimes a particular metal or mineral is so dominant in a sample that it can exclude many geographical areas. The search however needs to be centered on places that are related to the bones in question or the search is too broad and futile. It will take a few days for us to reach a definitive analysis of this earth sample. In the meantime, I would recommend that you take ground samples at the location where the skeletal remains were found. Also look into other addresses where the residents of the house in question may have resided in the last five to seven years. There is no evidence of bone rot. In an adult bone rot takes many years. However, bones of a newborn child are less dense and more quickly susceptible to breaking down. It would be fair to assume that these skeletal remains were buried in the ground less than two years."

Round Corners

Chapter Fourteen

The examination of the skeletal remains by Dr. Malcolm ended just before ten-thirty. He had to cross the city to Harvard University to teach a class at Noon. Plus the lab was getting busy. Other members of the forensic laboratory had started examining a body that had been retrieved from a long cold slab that lined one of the walls of the room. And a half hour earlier, attendants had brought in the body of an elderly man that Bill Normandin overheard had been found in an alley behind the Catholic Cathedral.

When the conversations of the examiners began to indicate that they were about to open the body in order to ascertain the contents of his stomach, Bill indicated to Rubin, "I think I better leave the room before I get sick." Dr. Malcolm, aware of the detective's condition, stated: "Let's bring this examination to a close. I will assign members of the staff to do studies on the bones and to determine the mineral components of the dirt that we have collected. Rubin, in a few days I should be able to send you the results of these studies. In the meantime, I would start collecting earth samples from the vicinity of where these bones were discovered as well as other places frequented by the members of that household."

The weather had worsened with ominous dark clouds moving in from the south. The rain was light and felt warmer than earlier in the morning. "Let's make a quick visit to my family in Newton," said David. "I'm not sure who will be home but looking at this sky I don't think we should wait to have dinner with the family before returning to New Bedford."

The Rubin residence was situated on a curving side street. The homes were mostly made of red brick. "This is quite a different type of neighborhood from the ones I'm familiar," commented Bill.

"My father who specializes in the cutting of precious gems purchased it through friends he knew in Manhattan. The rabbi of our synagogue had become aware from his contacts that a "nice Yiddish" family was looking to move into the city," chuckled David.

Bill rushed behind David into the entrance of the house as the wind and rain had intensified. David Rubin was greeted at the door by his grandfather who kissed each other on both cheeks. The old man with a long gray beard held David at a distance and said, "Look at you, all grown up. And I notice you still have the long hair hanging down your back. Such a look!"

David introduced Bill to his grandfather, "Grandfather, this is Detective William Normandin of the New Bedford Police Department." David's grandfather grabbed both of Bill's hands in his and said, "Welcome to our home." He replaced the yamaka that had slipped to the side during these exuberant greetings. "Come, come. Your mother and sister are in the kitchen preparing our dinner."

The greetings in the kitchen were loud and joyful until David announced, "I think it would be wise for Bill and I to return to New Bedford as soon as possible. The skies are menacing." David's mother exclaimed, "But we haven't seen you in such a long time and looked at what we have prepared. Everyone will be so disappointed." David's sister, Augusta, came to his rescue, "I just heard on the radio that a powerful storm is approaching Long Island and seems to be moving very quickly. A weatherman is comparing this storm to the one that devastated the southern facing coastline a few years ago. He referred to it as the hurricane of 1938."

David's mother finally agreed to their departure but only on the condition that the young men sit down at the kitchen table and enjoy some of the food they were preparing. "We'll also make up two baskets to take with you."

David and Bill left the Rubin's Newton residence in a heavy rain. David took some time to adjust the electric motor at the top of the windshield that controlled the wipers on the driver's side of the small white truck. "It seems to be working better," commented David. "If the rain and wind increases as predicted, let's hope the wipers do their job." "At least we have daylight," added Bill. "That should be better than the darkness we had earlier this morning."

By four o'clock the young men had reached the outskirts of Taunton. The wind and rain had indeed increased in velocity. They had encountered some tree branches that were scattered on the roads. They continued cautiously and made steady progress. Around Lakeville they encountered a police road block. The officer in a heavy rain coat and hat approached the white van. He informed David, "There's a tree that has fallen about a quarter of a mile ahead that is blocking the road. What are you doing on the roads? Aren't you aware that a storm with hurricane force winds is just south of the Cape and Islands?" David explained that his companion was a New Bedford Police detective and that he was a member of the local coroner's office. "We are trying to return to our area in the hopes of being able to provide some assistance," explained David.

"I see," commented the officer. "Follow me. There's a dirt road that skirts the blocked road. I'll get you on the main road again and hopefully you'll make it to your destination."

After avoiding large puddles and muddy areas on the dirt road, David waved to the Officer as they continued on Route 18 now only about twenty miles from the center of New Bedford. It took the travelers close to an hour to reach the outskirts of New Bedford. Bill Normandin suggested, "I would take Acushnet Avenue to the center of the city. It's on higher ground. Belleville Avenue near the mills that line the river floods easily when rains are heavy."

Two weary young men drove into the parking lot of the central police department on Union Street. The police station was a beehive of activity. Reports and directions were being passed along from one office to another. Just as David and Bill entered Inspector O'Malley's office, the electric lights flickered and then suddenly all was in darkness. Some daylight darkened by heavy clouds was still entering the room.

O'Malley was on the telephone. A second later he put the receiver back down on its on cradle. Looking up at the young men, he lamented, "We have now lost our telephone connection. I had expected that you would stay in the Boston area until the storm was over. Since you are here we can surely use your help."

"Fortunately, the weather men are now indicating that the storm has veered out to the east and away from our coastline. It looks like we will escape the strong storm surge coming directly into our harbor that destroyed more than sixty percent of our fishing fleet during the "38" hurricane," stated O'Malley. "David, I think, the best service you could provide the city is to assist at St. Luke's Hospital." David Rubin agreed with O'Malley's recommendation.

O'Malley then suggested to Bill Normandin, "Go to the dispatch desk. The Chief is looking for all the support he can get to alert people along the shore front to leave their boats once they are secured and seek higher ground. We may be missing a direct hit from the storm but there is still a lot of fury in its winds that will affect the city. Please be careful, especially of any electric lines lying across the streets."

Round Corners

Book Three

Round Corners

Book Three

Chapter Fifteen

Catching up with the past:

Chief Homicide Inspector, Daniel O'Malley, was following up on the most recent development in the death of the tailor, Gabriel Beaumont. The acknowledgement by Mr. Anthony Willard, President of the Whaling City National Bank, that his chauffeur had driven the tailor to his residence in the north end of the city was a game changer. When he entered Roland LaPorte's insurance office on the avenue, the bell attached above the door rang announcing his arrival. Roland exited his private office located to the rear of the storefront office. The secretary's desk in the front room was empty. Roland greeted O'Malley, "Good morning, Inspector." O'Malley recognized that even though Roland seemed composed, signs of anxiety and fear were evident in his eyes.

"Please, come to my office," welcomed Roland. As they entered the office O'Malley became aware that another person was in the room. He recognized him. It was Attorney David Beauchamp. The attorney was well-known in legal circles. He had been around for many years and his unkempt dress masked a sharp legal mind.

The attorney stood while O'Malley and he exchanged greetings. O'Malley was a bit surprised that his meeting with Roland was taking on a very formal tone. True, the day previously he had asked Officer William Normandin to announce his wish to meet with Roland. This had given Roland time to prepare for the interview.

Roland invited the Inspector to take a chair around the small coffee table. They sat across from each other and attorney Beauchamp was to one side but evidently just a bit closer to Roland. O'Malley intuited the orchestration of the grouping to favor Roland LaPorte.

Attorney Beauchamp began the conversation, "I understand that some new information in the death of Gabriel Beaumont has come forth. Mr. LaPorte has sought my assistance."

Inspector O'Malley took advantage of this opening to begin his interview. "Two new pieces of evidence place Mr. Beaumont at the home of your...may I say client, Roland LaPorte." O'Malley had directed the statement to the attorney. It was already evident that Roland had been instructed not to speak without the attorney's consent.

O'Malley continued, "A source known to your client, Al Lepage, provided information that places Gabriel Beaumont in his attic room at the LaPorte residence on the weekend in question. The LaPorte's had graciously given to Mr. Lepage and his wife, who was expecting their first child, a small dresser a few weeks earlier. In a concealed compartment of one of the drawers, Al had discovered a small envelope that contained the winnings of a bet that Beaumont had made on the previous Friday. As you know from the newspapers Mr. Beaumont's body was discovered on the broken pier behind the Revere early on Monday Morning. The envelope with the date of the bet and the winnings was freely given to Roland a few days ago." O'Malley looked over to Roland whose face portrayed neither acknowledgement nor denial of the statement.

While O'Malley continued introducing his evidence, David Beauchamp took out an already filled corn cob pipe, lit it and began to fill the room with a pleasant tobacco aroma. Holding his pipe in his left hand while a juicy spot appeared in the corner of his lips, the attorney queried, "You mentioned two new pieces of evidence had come forward. Would you please present the details of the other situation?"

O'Malley continued knowing that this was totally new information that was being presented. Also at this time in the investigation he wished to keep the identity of this source confidential. "A person has come forward who states that he dropped off Gabriel Beaumont at his residence, the LaPorte's home, very late on the Sunday evening only a few hours prior to the discovery of his body."

Attorney Beauchamp jumped on this statement, "May I inquire as to the identity of this person?" O'Malley answered courteously, "Not at this moment in our investigation. If and when your client is charged in connection with Mr. Beaumont's death, as you know well, all this material will be shared with Roland's defense attorney. At this moment we are curious as to what Roland has to say about these assertions made by two different sources. Roland has become a person of interest in this case."

Attorney Beauchamp quickly glanced at Roland and then addressed O'Malley, "I have advised Mr. LaPorte to refrain from entering into such discussions." O'Malley answered, "That is his prerogative. I do, however, have one request. May we have his permission to make another search of his home? We could easily get a warrant to do this search. Again as you are well aware, Mr. Beauchamp, we are not bringing any charges against Roland whom you have evidently agreed to represent. We are pursuing our investigation following up on recent and new evidence."

Round Corners

Chapter Sixteen

Inspector O'Malley waited in the front office while Attorney Beauchamp conferred with Roland LaPorte. Beauchamp asked Roland, "The Inspector stated that your home has already been searched." Roland answered, "That is true. Inspector O'Malley himself conducted the first search of Gabriel Beaumont room just a few days after his body was found. On another occasion he sent two investigators to search Gabriel's room and my wife Michelle allowed them to view the rest of our home."

Beauchamp questioned Roland, "Were you informed that anything was uncovered at the time of those searches?" "No," answered Roland. "After the second search the Inspector informed us that Gabriel's room that he had previously instructed my wife and me to leave intact could be used as we wished."

Attorney Beauchamp opened the door of Roland's office and informed O'Malley that, "In a spirit of cooperation, we have reluctantly agreed that you may conduct another and hopefully final search of the LaPorte residence."

Inspector O'Malley thanked the attorney. "Please inform Mr. & Mrs. LaPorte that the search of the home will occur within the hour."

Upon entering his unmarked police car, O'Malley immediately called the main precinct. Earlier that morning and prior to leaving his office O'Malley had already put into place orders for a search of the LaPorte home. He had instructed Officer Bill Normandin to conduct the search. "Remember, Bill, our previous searches were conducted hoping to find a reason as to why Gabriel Beaumont had been killed. Now, you will be viewing the LaPorte home as the possible scene of the crime. The evidence you are seeking could be quite different including an instrument used to inflict the stroke that brought on Gabriel's death. You have not participated in the prior searches. I am hoping you will bring fresh eyes and your keen instincts to this search. You have proven to me that, even without official training, you have an uncanny ability as a detective."

Around eleven o'clock, Officer Bill Normandin was knocking at the front door of the LaPorte home. Michelle greeted him warmly but Bill noticed that she was shaking. Following the instructions given by O'Malley, the officer asked Michelle to accompany him. He had different size paper bags with him that was to be used to collect any possible evidence.

Officer Normandin had been a part of this neighborhood since his birth. He was somewhat familiar with the house. As a young boy his mother had sent him to pick up some of the cough drop lozenges that Michelle made in her basement kitchen. He suggested, "Let's start the visit in the basement where you make your very popular medication."

Officer Normandin had decided on an approach to the search. First, he would take a big view of each room. Prior to searching drawers or cabinets, looking under furniture or behind items, he thought he might see something out of place or odd. In the basement kitchen, he put two items in a paper bag. It was a screwdriver and a hammer. Both looked as if they had been used only on a rare occasion. He knew from reading the reports of the coroner that a small deep wound had been inflicted on the left temple of the victim.

Michelle quietly observed the officer. She said nothing and fingered her rosary beads. In the main kitchen, Officer Normandin bagged a knife sharpener from one of the drawers. It was a long piece of some type of stone with a handle. It had been used many times over the years. The tip was rounded and dull but approximately the size of the wound described by the coroner.

Finally, Michelle and Officer Normandin reached the attic floor where Gabriel Beaumont had his bedroom. Michelle's shaking from nervousness and fear became more noticeable. Officer Normandin felt sorry for her and almost wanted to hold her and comfort her. He quickly assumed his professional approach to his search. He entered the nearly empty attic room first and discovered nothing of interest. The rounded top trunk held only clothing and a few newspaper articles and pictures.

In the adjacent room that had served as Gabriel's room, Officer Normandin did a full 360 degrees circle in the center of the room. A stripped down bed with a thin mattress was near the center of the room. A small marbled top stand was to one side. He asked Michelle pointing to the other side of the bed "Is that where the dresser you gave to the Lepage family stood?" "Yes," she answered. Her throat was dry and the sound almost cracked as it left her mouth.

The small closet was empty. Well-ironed and thin curtains covered the single window in the room that faced the front of the building. Officer Normandin looked behind the curtains. He found nothing, not even dust. A single pull chain light hung from the ceiling. He pulled it and a dim light lit the room brightened by the sunlight coming in the window. As he left Gabriel's room, he observed the metal cross hanging on the wall adjacent to the door. Following Michelle onto the landing that led to the stairs, Officer Normandin came to an abrupt halt.

"Just wait here one minute, Mrs. LaPorte," stated Normandin. He re-entered the room. He looked up at the crucifix. In a flash he thought he had found what had killed Gabriel Beaumont. He carefully placed the crucifix in a paper bag and informed Michelle that he had taken it from the room, pointing to the bag. Suddenly Bill Normandin felt himself shaking with nervousness. He found himself breathing heavily. Together two very shaky persons came down from the attic bedroom.

Round Corners

Chapter Seventeen

Al Lepage entered the central precinct of the New Bedford police department. As instructed the prior evening in a telephone call from Chief Homicide Inspector Daniel O'Malley, Al informed the police officer at the desk that the Inspector had requested that he come to the station the following afternoon.

Al was asked to take a seat and that someone would be with him shortly. Al was very nervous. His wife, Janet, had tried to reassure him that he would do fine. All he needed to do was to share what he knew in his own simple way.

Inspector O'Malley introduced himself and asked Al Lepage to follow him to his office. O'Malley easily recognized Al's uneasiness, as he kept twisting the cap he held in his hands. "Mr. Lepage," started O'Malley, "my office is so pleased with the contributions you have made in the past assisting us in our attempt to solve the untimely death of Mr. Gabriel Beaumont. These prior statements have indirectly come to my attention. Now, we need to have your actual words recorded as potential evidence in a court of law."

"I have asked Mrs. Cummings to record in shorthand my questions and your responses. Let us review briefly your knowledge of this case."

"Did you personally know Mr. Gabriel Beaumont?" asked the Inspector.

Al Lepage answered, "Yes, I have known him for several years."

"Can you describe the meetings you may have had with Mr. Beaumont?" continued O'Malley.

Al began to relax; "I first met Gabriel at the home of my friends, Roland and Michelle LaPorte. Soon after his arrival from Canada, Gabriel opened a small tailor shop in the center of the city. Within the space of a few months, Mr. Beaumont approached me at a luncheonette. He had heard that I picked up numbers and wanted to place a bet with me. He has been my regular customer for over two years."

O'Malley quickly understood that he was in the presence of an honest and naïve young man. He needed to be careful. He would not want to be accused of leading this witness nor did he want to take any unnecessary advantage. "What information did you first bring to our attention?"

"The newspapers hadn't contained any information about the sixty dollar winning that I had delivered to Gabriel, the weekend of his death," answered Al. "I thought that information could be helpful in giving a reason for him getting killed. Plus, I was told that my identity would be kept secret."

"Did you provide any other information about this case?" asked O'Malley.

"I related to Officer Bill Normandin that I had found a small envelope with these winnings including the date and the number wagered in a small hidden compartment of a dresser the LaPortes had given to my wife and me," stated Al.

"Why did that seem important to you?" asked O'Malley.

"The word on the streets and in the newspapers was that Gabriel never came home that weekend. When I approached Roland LaPorte about this, he became threatening." Al looked pleadingly at the Inspector, "All of a sudden, out of a fear for my wife who is expecting our first baby, I wondered if I had stepped into something that was way beyond me. Life, for me, has always been pretty straightforward.

However, Officer Normandin reassured me that he would be watchful for our safety. I've known him and his family for many years now and I've learned that I can trust him."

Inspector O'Malley inquired, "Is there anything else that you would wish to add to your testimony in reference to Gabriel Beaumont's death?"

Al shook his head in the negative and breathed out a sigh of relief. His call to appear at the police station wasn't as bad as he had imagined.

O'Malley commented, "Mr. Lepage, your testimony has been officially recorded." The Inspector thanked Mrs. Cummings and she left the office. "Before you leave, I wish to share a few thoughts with you. I am aware that it was your initial wish to have your identity kept secret. We will do all in our power to honor that wish. First, your testimony may never be used in a trial if the defendant, Mr. Roland LaPorte, enters a guilty plea. Also some cases are resolved with the judge accepting a plea bargain. In such cases much of the testimony recorded in putting together a case against a defendant is kept in the files and not exposed to the public."

"However," continued O'Malley, "once the case is handed over to the District Attorney, it is our duty as police detectives to provide him with the complete report of our investigation. The defense attorney for Mr. LaPorte is also made privy to all this information so that he is in the best position to build his defense."

Inspector Daniel O'Malley stood up from behind his desk and came in front of the still seated Al Lepage who moved to the edge of the chair wondering if the interview was over. "Mr. Lepage," observed O'Malley, "your assistance in this case has been very helpful. I am personally grateful that a fellow citizen has come forward with evidence knowing full well that he has exposed his own dealings that are unlawful. Again we will try our best to conceal your identity. I do have a word of advice. It would be in your best interest to discontinue your connection with illegal gambling. Officer Normandin informs me that you have a successful bread delivery business. I appreciate that present times are difficult. Maybe you can find other means to supplement your income that are within the law."

As the Inspector stepped back a few paces, Al stood and shook O'Malley hand. "Thank you for your advice," stated Al. "My wife has been encouraging me to do as you mentioned and we have a few thoughts in mind."

Round Corners

Chapter Eighteen

Inspector O'Malley met with Chief Peter Downey. O'Malley brought the chief up to date on the Gabriel Beaumont case. "In the search of the LaPorte residence just a few hours ago, Officer Normandin brought back a metal crucifix that hung on the wall of the tailor's bedroom. He suspected that it might be the murder weapon. Doctor Kendall concluded that it was such an instrument that would have created the deep indentation on the left side of Gabriel's temple. It compared perfectly with the measurements he had made in the lab."

O'Malley continued, "We have two witnesses who can place Gabriel Beaumont at the LaPorte home the night of his death. We have discovered an instrument in their residence that is most probably the murder weapon. Roland LaPorte made statements that he despised Gabriel. The LaPortes have two young children. What we have uncovered about Gabriel's propensity to be sexually involved with young children could easily have come to Roland's attention and was the tipping point that provided a motive or occasion to commit such an act."

Chief Downey thought a while and stated, "It's time we pull together the results of your investigation and present it to the District Attorney. This case has been lingering in the shadows for over six months now. Paul Clifford will need this information to prepare his case for court. In the meantime, bring in Roland LaPorte and book him on suspicion in the homicide of Gabriel Beaumont."

"When I met with Roland Laporte earlier this morning for an informal interview in his north end office, Roland had already employed David Beauchamp as his counsel," added O'Malley.

"All the more reason we be in contact with Paul Clifford as soon as possible. His office needs to be well prepared to go against the crafty, old attorney Beauchamp," stated the police chief.

Round Corners

Chapter Nineteen

At the initial court hearing, Attorney David Beauchamp negotiated with the District Attorney Paul Clifford that the charges be reduced to involuntary manslaughter. Attorney Beauchamp had convinced Roland LaPorte that it was in his best interest to relate the events that had led to Gabriel's death. This had been very difficult for Roland. He had hoped to keep this sordid episode from his wife, Michelle. How would she be able to accept the fact that her cousin, Gabriel, had attempted to molest her son, Paul, in their own home. And that when he came upon this situation, her husband in a moment of rage had struck and killed him.

However, the D.A. would not budge on the charges relating to the disposing of the body. The judge agreed that Roland LaPorte could be released on his personal recognizance.

Michelle LaPorte sat weeping in the courtroom while the legal procedures continued. Her neighbor and friend, Paulette, had accompanied her. Paulette reached out her hand and held Michelle's hand trying to comfort her. Michelle's mind was racing all over the place. At one moment she was recalling how her cousin Gabriel had come into their lives and feelings of anger surprised her. In the next moment she was looking forward, fearful and confused as to the future of her family. It surprised her that usually when situations were difficult, she would automatically turn to prayer. Now that feeling of comfort that normally came with the prayers of her rosary beads seem to grab at her throat. She sensed being abandoned by God and it brought dark thoughts of fright and aloneness.

Suddenly Roland LaPorte's hearing before the judge was over. In her confused state of mind, Michelle thought she had heard that an agreement had been reached as to when Roland should reappear before the court. Michelle and Roland met in the hallway outside the courtroom. They held each other and though Roland projected himself as self-confident, Michelle could feel a shaking in his body.

"David Beauchamp wants me to come to his office," Roland shared with Michelle. "I'll meet you at home as soon as our meeting is over." Michelle broke away reluctantly.

In the attorney's office, David Beauchamp quickly reviewed the morning procedures with his client. "There is a lot of sympathy in the courts and I suspect even more so in the public for your situation," started David. Roland confidence grew within him as he observed his attorney's bright mind picking his way through the moments of the hearing. "There is little or no sympathy for your wife's cousin," continued the attorney. "The fact that he can no longer endanger the well-being of young children is looked upon as a blessing. However, the killing of any person no matter how dangerous or despised is never taken lightly in our court of law. We achieved a major concession when the District Attorney agreed to a charge of involuntary manslaughter. However, the charge left standing of disposing of a human person concerns me. It may seem minor to most people but a jury of your peers would probably be led by the prosecution to see this as an act of cowardice but even worse premeditated."

Roland's earlier feelings of confidence in his attorney were now mixed with fear. "What do you think we should do?" inquired Roland.

"I've read over very carefully all the results of the investigation that were prepared by Inspector O'Malley and presented to me by the prosecutor," continued the attorney. What the attorney did not share with his client was that he learned from the inspector's notes that although Roland LaPorte was a respected businessman in the community, many of his neighbors and others in the community experienced him as being aloof and cold.

The attorney continued, "Also I am aware of the case of Robert Keenan who murdered his wife in a fit of rage when he learned that his son was most likely abused by Gabriel. As you know he has already been sentenced to Walpole State Prison for a period of twenty years. His case is very different from yours but it centers on the same person, Gabriel Beaumont. There could be a sense in the community of sweeping all this together in one brush and getting it behind them. A jury can be very fickle and can easily be led by a good prosecutor. The District Attorney has decided to prosecute this case himself. I believe he senses that the conclusion of the Beaumont saga will provide him political capital."

"My recommendation to you, Roland, is that we enter into a plea bargain with the prosecutor," continued David Beauchamp. Roland was confused. He hadn't anticipated this coming and wasn't sure what it meant to him. David took out his corn cob pipe, lit it and continued developing his plan.

"It is my suggestion," continued the attorney, "that we plead guilty to involuntary manslaughter and ask that the D. A. drop the charges in reference to the disposing of Gabriel's body. Plus, we will ask, under this plea bargain, that your time of incarceration not exceed three years."

Roland suddenly felt faint. The attorney observed this and quickly went on to the next point of his logic, "A sentence of less than three years allows you to be placed at the local Ash Street jail rather than being sent to a state prison further away from your family. I'm quite confident that we can get the district attorney and the sitting judge to agree to a sentence of eighteen months. I could ask for a period of six months in jail and the rest of the sentence to be served on probation."

"We will plead your case based on the fact that you are an outstanding citizen in the business community and that you have a family with two young children," continued the attorney. "Your children have suffered enough already. The court will not be pressing to bring more hardship into their lives. Also the D. A. will have his conviction and the case will be closed."

"Please consider this carefully," cautioned the attorney. "Confide this with your wife, Michelle, and let me know your decision. Don't take too long. I don't want the District Attorney Paul Clifford to get too far ahead in his prosecutorial tactics so that he is reluctant to agree with our plea. I would like to take him by surprise."

Round Corners

Chapter Twenty

Roland LaPorte met with Attorney David Beauchamp early the next morning. His conversation with his wife, Michelle, the evening after the initial court hearing had been painful. Roland had been quite confident that this wise, old attorney would find mitigating circumstances in his case that would not necessitate any jail time.

Roland now realized that he was wrong. His cowardly action of disposing the body of Gabriel Beaumont was coming back to haunt him. Michelle was in shock. She could not appreciate the attorney's plan of pleading guilty. Roland had tried to explain, "Michelle, if a jury finds me guilty on some of the charges against me and the sentence is over three years then I would need to go to a state prison. The local county jail in New Bedford is limited to holding a person for periods of less than three years."

"What about the children?" asked Michelle. "How are they going to handle you're going to prison?"

"If I am nearby, they will be able to come to visit with me," explained Roland. "I know that they are young and as much as I would like to shield them from all these scary scenarios, all of us need to face them together. My pride has brought this upon you and the children. Now all I can do is ask you and them to share this burden with me. I'm so sorry that I've brought this on you, Michelle. I'm pleading with you to be strong for all of us."

Also in his mind, Roland had concluded that his local presence would enable him to keep an eye on his insurance business even while in the local jail. He knew that he couldn't share these thoughts right now with Michelle. They were too cold and business like. He was beginning to appreciate that his former attention to business matters had made him blind to the personal needs of his wife and children.

Michelle finally agreed to the attorney's plan to plead guilty to limited charges and to strike a deal for a limited sentence and hopefully to serve most of it on probation.

Attorney David Beauchamp was sitting behind his desk when Roland entered. In contrast to the unkempt appearance of his clothing and hair, the material on David's desk was quite orderly. Roland reflected that it probably had something to do with the attorney's orderly mind that seemed to assess matters quickly and placed them in proper sequence. Roland had tried to convince himself that he needed to trust his attorney. This was a strange phenomenon for Roland who consulted with few people and almost exclusively trusted only his own inner reasoning. As little as it seemed, the appearance of the attorney's orderly desk helped to build Roland's trust in the attorney.

"Hopefully, the district attorney's schedule will allow me to meet with him today," stated David Beauchamp. "I will put forth our proposal. I'm sure that he will want to meet with you to assure himself that you are in agreement. I know the district attorney well enough that he will want to negotiate terms that places him in the lead of these negotiations. You just listen carefully. My presentation may seem weak at times but I'm quite sure that he will come close to our plan but will think that he authored it."

"Sitting there quietly is very difficult for me," said Roland. "I appreciate that," answered the attorney. He continued, "Our next hearing before the judge is less than two weeks away. My hope is that we will have pulled this all together before then and that the district attorney and I are in a position to put our plan before the judge that day. I will want your wife, Michelle, and the children in the court.

The success of my plan rests heavily on the sympathy of the judicial system. Too many children have been negatively impacted by Gabriel Beaumont. Our proposal before the court will help bring this case to a conclusion."

Round Corners

Chapter Twenty-one

Meanwhile Nurse Patricia Flynn was all excited as she came on her assigned floor at St. Luke's Hospital. She couldn't wait to speak with Nurse Deolinda DeSouza who was the nurse in charge of the floor. She tried to contain herself until all the assignments of the nursing staff and updates on the condition of the patients were discussed by the team.

Patricia had been assigned to nine patients at the end of the west wing. She found most of the patients resting comfortably and a few early birds were preparing themselves for their breakfast. When she went back to the desk area to prepare the medications that were soon to be administered, she found Dee sitting alone reviewing charts. Two of the doctors had already made their rounds and had entered some notes to the patients' records.

"Can we get together later?" asked Nurse Flynn. "There are some new developments in the situation of young John Keenan that I would like to share with you."

Nurse DeSouza answered, "I'll be by to see you when I'm free. You have piqued my curiosity."

About an hour later Nurse Deolinda DeSouza went to the west wing of her floor. When Nurse Flynn saw her supervisor standing at the door of the patient's room, she excused herself. "I'll be right back," she said, "puffing up the pillow behind Mr. Winslow who was recovering well from the surgery that had removed several toes on his left foot."

Nurse Dee invited Pat to come to the end of the hall. They looked out the window that overlooked the entrance to the emergency room.

An ambulance was parked near the entrance but otherwise all was quiet out there this morning. The sun shone brightly casting long shadows of the three story hospital building as far as across the nearby street. Soon the sun would be high in the heavens and another hot and humid day would descend on the city. One could expect this toward the end of July. "It's going to be a hot one," commented Nurse Dee. Then turning to Pat she asked, "And what's the latest on John Keenan."

"As you know I've been visiting with him at his new home in Swansea on weekends," started Patricia. "Lately it's been every second or third weekend. He has been settling in quite well with Mr. and Mrs. Stevens. He's up every day. Although he rarely speaks, he does acknowledge what is being said to him by either a nod of agreement or a frown on his face. This past month he has taken to going outdoors. He has become fascinated with the few animals the Steven's have on their large property. He is assisting in feeding the chickens and loves to be near the two small goats who greet him with "ma" sounds. We have seen bright smiles on his face."

"Oh, that's just great," said Dee. "I'm so happy for him."

"But that's not all," continued Patricia. "Mrs. Stevens asked me if I might know some young children who might come to visit with John. Her husband, whom you know is a retired doctor, thought it would be good to reintroduce him to other children. I immediately thought of your two nieces. And when I mentioned to Mrs. Stevens that they were the daughters of the police inspector, she thought that it would provide the needed privacy for this situation. She felt assured that the O'Malley's would be circumspect and professional. Other persons unfamiliar with John's trauma at seeing his father beat his mother to death could easily become morbidly curious and negatively impact their children. I assured her that your sister- in-law would know how to handle this meeting of the children."

"Maria and I are getting together later on this evening,' stated Dee. "Once a month we gather with a few other women trying to find a solution to family violence and protecting the children and women who live in such circumstances. My husband who is a lawyer wrote a draft of a law that would empower the police to intervene and arrest an abusive husband. However, except for our local congressman only one other representative on the north shore signed onto the bill. The bill will die before it can be presented to the floor of the house. The present session of congress ends in a few days."

"I'll share this invitation with her. Julia and Margaret are delightful young girls who are filled with such curiosity and excitement. They could very well be what the doctor ordered," commented Dee with a smile.

Round Corners

Chapter Twenty-two

On an early Tuesday morning in August, Maria O'Malley was driving to the rural town of Swansea. Nurse Patricia Flynn sat in the front seat of the family Model T Ford. The O'Malley's two girls, Julia and Margaret, sat very prim and proper in the back seat.

The fog that enveloped the area was beginning to lift. It was promising to be a hot and rather humid day. Pat was providing directions to Maria on how to reach the Stevens property. She had been visiting young John Keenan for over four months now. In the weeks immediately following John's release from the hospital, Nurse Patricia Flynn had been picked up at her home every weekend and chauffeured to Swansea. Under Pat's watchful and tender care during John's hospital stay, John had begun to retreat from his deep traumatic coma. When John's father, Bob Keenan, had learned that his son had been sexually molested by Gabriel Beaumont, he took out his anger on his wife. Bob had not appreciated that his son was being tutored in the French language. John's father had been convicted of beating his wife to death in John's presence. Doctor Peterson, who had managed John Keenan's care at St. Luke's Hospital, had conferred with the Stevens and all agreed that some continuity of care would be helpful.

In order to reach Swansea one had to cross through the neighboring mill city of Fall River. As they approached the top of President Avenue, Patricia turned to the two girls in the back seat. "Hold on," she pointed out to the front of the vehicle which was now beginning to descend, "this will be quite an exciting ride." What made the ride especially interesting was that as the descent progressed, each cross street leveled off, before the street proceeded down again. There were five such intersections.

Julia and Margaret held their breaths as they proceeded down the hilly street and then suddenly they found themselves being pushed back into their seats as the car reached a cross road. They screamed with joy. What was most exciting is that it kept on happening as they proceeded to the bottom of the hill. "Wow," screamed Julia and Margaret. Julia asked, "Are we coming back home this way? This is so much fun."

Her mother Maria answered, "Unfortunately, the ride back home will make this road a steep climb uphill and that's not as exciting. Plus many people avoid this hill that puts quite a strain on the engine. And it requires great coordination on the part of the driver's feet." She pointed to the pedals on the floor below her. The girls stood up and glancing over the back of the driver's seat saw most of the pedals that their mother described. However, their mother's flowing skirt concealed the left one from view. "There are three of them. The left one is the clutch, the one in the middle is the brake and the one to the right is the gas pedal. Your father is very good at easing the clutch and putting pressure on the gas so as not to roll back. That gets me nervous, so I will avoid this street on the way home. There is a street further east that avoids this steep hill."

Not long afterwards, the O'Malley Model T turned onto a long driveway bordered by tall evergreens. They came to a circle in front of a spreading two story wooden house with many gables. One could hear the rocks being spread by the tires as they proceeded to the front door.

The chauffeur, Thomas Applebee, greeted them at the front entrance. "It is so good to see you, Miss Flynn," he said as he opened his arms in welcome to the rest of the group.

"This is Mrs. O'Malley and her two daughters, Margaret and Julia," announced Patricia Flynn.

"Come follow me," stated the chauffeur as he led them through the house to a screened in porch at the back of the house. Margaret

74

spoke to her younger sister, "Look at how high the ceilings are and the curving stairway that goes upstairs." Maria O'Malley had also observed the grandeur and yet simplicity that Nurse Patricia Flynn had told her had been the Stevens' summer home. Now that Doctor Peter Stevens had retired from his medical practice at Children's Hospital in Boston, they had made this small farm their residence.

Mrs. Elizabeth Stevens was sitting in a cushioned wicker chair reading a book. Young John Keenan was standing looking out of the screened porch toward a small pond. Mrs. Stevens turned to greet her guest. She stood and welcomed them to join her at a small table. "I'm sure you are thirsty from your trip. It's promising to be hot and humid. We have some lemonade for the young people as well as some iced tea."

As she poured the cool liquid for her guest, Elizabeth who had previously instructed Patricia that she preferred being addressed by her first name, inquired, "John would you also wish to have a drink?"

John turned to the group behind him. His eyes slowly surveyed the room. He had heard young voices and was surprised that two young girls were present. Elizabeth Stevens had informed him previously that they would be receiving some guest. John came closer to the table and accepted a glass of lemonade. "John," started Elizabeth, "these two young ladies visiting with us are Margaret and Julia. They are interested in visiting the animals on our little farm. Would you be so kind as to bring them to the animal area on the other side of the barn?"

John nodded and started for the rear screen door that led to the barn. Margaret quickly reminded her younger sister, Julia, to take her large brim hat. Julia had inherited the red hair and fair skin of her Nana, O'Malley, while Margaret resembled her mother with her dark hair and olive complexion. Even though Margaret was less than two years older than her sister, she had always watched carefully over her younger sibling.

John looked back and when the two girls started to make their way to follow him, he opened the screened door allowing them to proceed ahead of him. "Come this way," John spoke his first words to the girls. "We have chickens just behind the barn." When they approached the enclosure where about two dozen chickens were kept, John grabbed some cracked corn from a container. He offered some to the girls. "Just watch the chickens come up to the fence when you throw them some feed," John exclaimed. Sure enough the chickens came clucking, scratching and eating the corn spread near the fence.

Margaret exclaimed, "They sure keep moving around don't they." John answered, "Yes, most of the time chickens keep busy. Occasionally, you'll find one sitting in a dug out area in the dirt." He pointed to one to the side of a small ramp that led into the shed.

Julia pointed to the small shed and asked, "Is that where they sleep at night?" "Yes, they do," said John. "They also go in there to lay their eggs. We have little square boxes on the side of the inner wall where they lay on fresh straw and after a while the chicken will come down looking very proud. That's when we usually find an egg lying on the straw."

"Would you like to see the inside of the shed?" asked John. Both girls answered in unison, "Yes. Please. Can we?"

John brought them over to the side door of the chicken house. "I'll open the door slowly and sush away any chickens that may be inside. We don't want them to escape into the yard. They are very difficult to catch. They can run, fly a bit and even peck away at us when we try to hold them." A few chickens that were milling around inside the shed went scampering down the ramp leading to the outer enclosure. John pointed out, "There's one chicken in that far box sitting on the straw, probably ready to lay an egg."

Margaret and Julia were all smiles. They were city girls and this was all new to them. "We have a few other animals," said John. "Would you like to see them?" "Oh, yes," chimed Julia.

Around the other side of the barn, three goats were in an enclosure. Some distance away another enclosure held a large pig with six little ones. John pointed to the piglets and proudly said, "These little pink pigs were born just a few months ago. They are already getting big. They spend lots of time each day sucking the milk from their mother."

When the young people only quickly glanced at the goats as they went straightaway to see the pigs, the goats started to chime in together calling out to their guest not forget them. "These guys can make a lot of noise," said John. He stroked the head of the large goat that was poking her head above the fence. "We have to be careful because goats like to bite," he stated. "Mr. Benson, the caretaker, who's also in charge of the farm, draws milk from this one every day." He pointed to the large udder under the goat. "I don't particularly like the taste. It's too strong for me."

Before they realized that so much time had passed, Elizabeth Stevens was calling out to John and the girls to return to the house. As they reached the porch, Mrs. Stevens explained that their visitors needed to return home.

"Will you come back to visit?" asked John. The girls looked to their mother, "Can we come back again?" "This has been so much fun," stated Julia. "I also learned where our eggs that we have on Sunday morning come from," stated Margaret. "If it's alright with Mrs. Stevens, I mean Elizabeth; we'll make plans to return." John was beaming when Elizabeth agreed.

Round Corners

Chapter Twenty-three

Six months later, Roland LaPorte had his day in court. Once the District Attorney Paul Clifford arrived at a basic agreement with Roland's attorney, David Beauchamp, the case was no longer a priority. The Judge placed the case on his docket for a Friday prior to a long weekend. From what he had received from the attorneys in their written briefs, Judge Thompson approximated that in less than a half hour he would close the case and be on his way with his wife to a much needed break. Mary Thompson had planned to spend the celebration of her fortieth wedding anniversary with her husband Donald in New York City.

She had made them reservations at The Hotel Taft on 7th Avenue and 50th Street. The highlight of the weekend was attendance at the Alvin Theater of the popular musical, Pal Joey, a collaborative effort between Richard Rodgers and Lorenz Hart. Mary had informed her husband, "It's the first musical based on a William Shakespeare play. It's the hilarious storyline of "The Comedy of Errors." Eddie Albert, who we enjoyed so much when he co-hosted "the Honeymooners" on the radio, plays a lead part. Last month our neighbor, Joanne Moffat, and I saw him at the State Theater in Hollywood's version of "Brother Rat" that also featured Ronald Reagan and Jane Wyman."

Except for a skinny and shabby dressed reporter with the press card inserted in the band of a worn black fedora, only Michelle LaPorte with her friend Paulette sat in the chamber. Michelle had not agreed to her children being present in the courtroom as Roland's attorney had recommended. Since the proceedings were no longer a jury trial, Attorney David Beauchamp readily accepted her decision.

At eleven o'clock sharp, Judge Donald Thompson was at the bench. The District Attorney Paul Clifford briefly presented the plea bargain of the defendant, Roland LaPorte. The Judge asked Roland one question, "Do you understand fully the agreement that your lawyer and the District Attorney have presented to me on your behalf?" Roland nodded in the affirmative. "Please state your decision out loud," informed the Judge. Roland spoke up, "Yes, Your Honor."

"In the case of the involuntary death of Gabriel Beaumont by Roland LaPorte, I accept your plea of guilty. You are sentenced for a period of fifteen months, three to be served at the local Ash Street Jail with one year probation," stated the Magistrate. The Judge brought down his gavel and was observed removing his robes as he left the courtroom. The proceeding had taken a little more than twenty minutes.

When Al Lepage went to Ben LaBonte's Pharmacy, Ben informed Al of the results of the court relative to Gabriel Beaumont. "Thank God, it's over," he exclaimed. "My head has been spinning just thinking of the possibility of standing up in court. But as my wife, Janet, helped me to realize, my anxiety is nothing compared to what Michelle is going through."

"Fortunately," continued Ben, "there's been only a brief coverage in the afternoon paper. It's the end of a sad chapter."

On his next bread delivery to the LaPorte family, Al nervously apologized to Michelle for his role in seeing that her husband, Roland, was sent to prison. With tears evident in her eyes, Michelle graciously and warmly held Al's hands, saying, "You are a good man, Al. Don't ever doubt that. We have all been wronged. I pray that we will all be stronger and better persons as we live out this time of our lives."

Al was so grateful for Michelle's understanding as well as her reaching out to comfort him. However, a question kept nagging into his thoughts, "Did life always follow a straight and narrow path? Did he need to become more open to crooked lines and round corners?"

Round Corners

Chapter Twenty-four

As customary Al Lepage's last stop before going home from his day delivering bread and pastries was Ben LaBonte's Pharmacy. After Inspector O'Malley words of caution, Al had stopped picking up numbers on his route and the wagers that were regularly placed with Ben in his back room laboratory. To his surprise Skully had accepted Al's decision without objection. However, he did remind Al, "You still have to make your payments for Boudreau's bread route and truck."

Al informed Skully, "Janet and I have come up with another source of income. I can purchase ten pound boxes of vanilla and chocolate cream-filled cookies wholesale. Janet will put them up into smaller packages of a dozen. On Saturdays my customers are usually looking to buy a treat for the family. Even in these tough times, most of my customers can afford to purchase these smaller packages. Last Christmas we tried a similar approach with ribbon candy. It went over well. I'll be sure to bring you the $10.00 each week."

Skully scratched his bald head and as usual dandruff flakes dropped onto his shoulders and the stuff on his desk. "It might be better to make the payments to Ben at the pharmacy. I have a new runner and he'll bring me the payments. You better come by for your gas purchases but keep out of my office. I don't want anyone in the police force who may get wind of your days as a bookie to come snooping around here."

As he drove up to the three-decker down the street from the pharmacy, Al saw his older sister Claudia sitting on the front stoop with her boyfriend, Paul LaMontagne. Al and Paul got along very well, even though in size and personality, both were quite different. Al was a small man just a few inches over five feet, quite muscular but on a small frame. As his name suggested, Paul was a mountain of a young man. He was just a little over six feet tall and big. There was some fat around his middle but his upper body was solid and muscular. Side by side they were quite the contrasting pair.

Al appreciated a good time and was extremely curious and inquisitive but focused mostly on his work and the care of his family. Paul was a free spirit. He always had another fun thing on his agenda and sought others to join him in these escapades. Claudia, who as one of the older sisters with a constantly growing number of siblings, greatly admired Paul's joie de vive that contrasted with the heavy responsibilities that had been so much a part of her young life.

Paul's father had operated a fairly successful bar and grill in the Lepage's original hometown of Acushnet until Prohibition came on the scene. During those years it continued to serve home cooked meals to mill workers but without a ready access to bootleg liquor the grill hardly supported the family. With the repeal of Prohibition, business resumed but it faced more competition. Paul's father and his older brother, David, changed the character of the business into a night club. It was called The Barn which it had been just a few years prior. The evening entertainment on weekends included a local four piece orchestra and it slowly evolved with singers and other entertainers being added to the list. The weekend offering of clam cakes and fried clams became extremely popular and brought in a steady crowd to watch the show and wash down the salty, fried items with cold drafts of beer. When scantily clad dancers and singers were added, the family atmosphere changed and The Barn became mostly an all men's club.

"I was talking to Claudia about travelling to New York City," started Paul as Al joined them on the stoop. "Why don't you and Janet come with us?" asked Paul. "The World's Fair is in its second year and will be closing down in a few months. It's the only chance of our lifetime." Al countered, "I have a bread route to run, six days a week plus money is limited, especially now that we have our little girl, Charlotte." Paul knew that he had little chance of getting Claudia's parents' permission allowing her to go with him to New York alone, without another couple. Paul persisted in his plans for them. "Your brother Claude could run the bread route for a couple of days. I was thinking that we could leave early on a Friday morning and return by Sunday evening. That would give us a full day at the Fair to view the exhibits. I've been told that the General Motors pavilion called Futurama depicts life into the 1960's. The Transportation Zone includes the Ford Exposition that has a 100 foot turntable demonstrating the process by which its cars are built. RCA exhibit features television."

Knowing that he had piqued Al's curious nature, Paul continued with his "piece de resistance", "The Continental Baking Company building is dotted with red, blue and yellow balloons just like those on the wrappers of Wonder Bread. And the Borden building has a massive revolving platform that mechanically milks cows."

"Enough," interrupted Al. "Let me talk with Janet. I know she's been reading about the Fair and I'm sure she would love it. It's just that we have to make sure we can afford it." Looking to Claudia, "Do you think one of your sisters would look after Charlotte?" Claudia answered with a smile, "They'll be fighting over who will be caring for her."

On a Friday in August 1940, Paul was driving his father's Oldsmobile out of town with Al in the front seat and Claudia and Janet in the rear. The furthest Al and Janet had ever travelled was a visit to one of Janet's cousin near Springfield. Paul was all excited, "Off we go!" Claudia and Janet had prepared a large basket of food for the trip. It included sandwiches, a salad, cherries and peaches. Paul had assured them that they could get drinks along the way. In her careful study of the Fair in preparation for the trip, Janet had discovered that temporary housing had been built adjacent to Flushing Meadows to accommodate visitors to the Park. Claudia had made reservations for the four of them.

Round Corners

Chapter Twenty-five

The visitors from New Bedford were at the gate of the fairgrounds before it opened at 9 a.m. The price of general admission was 75 cents for adults. In her careful study of the World's Fair pamphlet, Janet had learned that the Fair itself was divided into zones. The Trylon and Perisphere served as a focal point around which were the Transportation, The Communications, The Production and Distribution and The Food zones. These exhibit buildings closed at 10 p.m. The Amusement area just east of these zones that covered about one-third of the fair's grounds stayed open until 2 a.m. The Government Zone also referred to as the foreign section was located at the north end of the fairgrounds.

The evening before Janet had suggested, "Let's plan our day. There is no way we will be able to see all the exhibitions. Let's make a list of what particularly appeals to each one of us. And with the help of the map of the fairgrounds, let's plan a route that will keep us from going around in circles and wasting time."

Everyone agreed. Al immediately asserted, "I'd like to see the Wonder Bread and dairy farm exhibits." Claudia suggested, "The Futurama exhibit with its moving chairs with individual loudspeakers seems to capture the theme of the Fair which is a vision of the world of tomorrow. That's my choice." Paul indicated, "My preference is visiting the Ford Exposition and the Aviation Building." Janet pointed out, "We will be entering the interior of the Theme Center on the world's largest escalator a portion of the way up the 700-foot Trylon. Then we will be directed into the Perisphere to view a diorama of a planned urban and exurban complex of the future. We have to allow time in our schedule for these initial exhibits."

Janet furthered pointed out, "The exhibits that Al wants to see are in what is called the Food Zone. That's where we will find many food concessions."

All agreed that they wanted to go to the amusement area after visiting other areas of the park since it stayed opened later than the others. Paul added, "I'd like to see Dream of Venus Building and the synchronized swimming show called, the Aquacade that is located in the amusement area near Fountain Lake." Claudia chuckled, "Paul, you are true to form. I understand Esther Williams is frequently featured."

Janet finally made her recommendation, "Before we go to the amusement area, I would like to visit some of the Government Zone. Last year over 60 nations were represented including places like Great Britain, Chile, Ireland, France and Japan, as well as a building representing the League of Nations. Last year prior to the Soviet Union signing a treaty with Hitler, their pavilion was a great attraction with its giant tower supporting the 79-foot high statue of the ideal worker, holding a star. Since then the Soviet pavilion has been taken down and replaced with a space known as the "American Common.""

The group had a great time together. One or the other kept pointing out, "Look at that!" as theatrical exhibits produced visions of leisure and efficiency through automation. Borden's Dairy World of Tomorrow was more spectacular than Al expected. "They can wash, dry and mechanically milk 150 pedigreed cows in a constant rotation." And leave it to Paul, while viewing exhibits in the foreign country area he found the Manchurian pavilion that included the Lama Temple. A huckster was calling people to view the charming young ladies, "Once a year the young lama is tested in his resolve to remain a celibate Buddhist priest. Courtesans and beautiful young dancers from the outside world try to seduce him from his holy way of life. Now ladies, this show has been approved by Good Housekeeping, but in case a stray moron seeking a racy spicy girl show is in this otherwise obviously intellectual audience, he too can go in there and not know the difference. But you, lovers of art will surely recognize this show to be the apogee of oriental choreography. This being the last show of the day, I am going to cut the price of admission in half."

The next morning Paul suggested that they go to Sunday Mass at St. Patrick's Cathedral. From there they made a quick visit to Rockefeller Center before heading back home. Paul had already visited New York City with some friends and was an excellent guide. Al did most of driving home once they left the confines of the city. Paul slept and snored in the adjacent front seat. He had had a few drinks prior to leaving the fairgrounds the night before.

Round Corners

Book Four

Round Corners

Book Four

Chapter Twenty-six

Setting the stage:

After graduating from St. Anthony's High School, Martha Lepage received word that made her dreams come true. She had been accepted into the three year nursing program at St. Luke's Hospital. At the orientation in August of 1939, prior to officially starting the program in early September, she met other young women from New Bedford and neighboring towns.

Director of Nursing, Miss Beverly Harrison, welcomed the 15 new students. This brought the freshman class up to 30. Fifteen students had started in May. "As you know, you will be moving into this building on September 9th. This building is known as the White Home and it will be your home for the next three years. Your program consist of a full three years, so that if by reason of illness, family emergency and similar situation results in missing a day of your education and training, those days are added on to the end prior to completing the requirements for graduation. Apart from our classrooms, dining facility and recreation room, this building is a residence for women. Men are not allowed beyond the waiting area adjacent to the front desk, except for our facility manager, Mr. Alfred Desautels."

Miss Harrison introduced three other, mostly white haired, women who were standing to her right. They were members of the teaching and supervisory staff. To her left she introduced two young women dressed in grey striped uniforms. They were members of the two upper classes. "We are all here to assist you in becoming a highly qualified medical professional. Most days will consist of class work where teachers and books will instruct you in the exceptional mystery of the human anatomy. You will also learn about the illnesses and injuries that disrupt this smooth running organism. The medical profession has dedicated itself to the discovery of the sources of illness and offers treatments and medication that assist in bringing relief to such maladies. Surgery, with the aid of anesthesia, provides ever new assistance in overcoming the many wounds that our fragile yet resilient bodies receive in our contact with the world of work and play."

Miss Harrison continued, "Every day of your training, you will first observe and then assist in the various wards of the hospital. You will rotate and be exposed to serving in all types of medical care from maternity, pediatric, emergency, even the pathology lab. You will soon learn that the B wards in the hospital are for women patients and the C wards are for men. Male orderlies are present on the C ward and provide for the male patients' personal care. As nurses we provide direct medical treatment and medication, plus supervise the orderlies."

"We will take a break now. Your upper class members will now show you through our building. Your room has already been assigned to you. Take this opportunity to meet your classmates and those who will share your room," continued Nurse Harrison. "After your tour we will gather at the dining facility for tea. At that time you will receive a list of the items you are required and allowed to bring with you on September 9th. Following tea an upper class member will escort you, in groups of no more than two, through the hospital areas. It is important that we do not disturb the patients or disrupt the medical staff in their care of the patients. Your warm, youthful smiles will provide your first medical treatment to our patients. Be on your way."

Martha was introduced to her roommate, Barbara O'Toole. An upper class nursing student showed them to their room. It was on the second floor of the west wing. Barbara was a rather petite and pretty woman. "Do you have any preference as to what side of the room will be yours?" asked Martha. Neither showed any preference so they decided based on who stood closest to what bed. Barbara exclaimed as she looked out of their window, "Oh, I will love the view of the sun as it sets over those maple trees. This will be a lovely room."

Martha observed that Barbara had an intriguing smile and a slight accent. Martha inquired, "Where do you come from?" "My family lives on the outskirts of Taunton," answered Barbara. "It's a small home on about two acres of land. There are many dairy farms in our section of town. My father works for Reed & Barton. It is one of the many silversmithing operations that are famous in Taunton. That's why Taunton is commonly known as the "Silver City". My mother works at one of the millinery shops in the center of town. I have one brother, Sean, who is two years younger than me."

As they made their way to the dining room for tea, Martha giggled, "I come from a very different background. We live in the north end of New Bedford, in a neighborhood of three-deckers. My father tends bar. My mother is at home watching over my many brothers and sisters. Only my oldest brother is married. Al lives with his wife Janet and their two little girls on the third floor of our tenement house. My sister Claudia is expecting to get engaged soon. In the meantime I share a room with three sisters. Our room is on the west side of our building but the view consists of the three story tenement house just a few feet away. It may take some adjustment for me to get used to all this space."

Over tea Martha and Barbara met other students in their class both those who had come for this orientation and the other students who had begun their studies in May. It was a lively group and both young women felt very comfortable and at ease. After a tour of the hospital, Martha met Barbara's mother who had gone shopping in downtown New Bedford while waiting for her daughter. Before entering the family car for the ride back to Taunton, Martha enthusiastically hugged Barbara. "I'll see you in a couple of weeks. I can't wait to get started. It all seems so much fun and exciting." Barbara who wasn't accustomed to this type of exuberance, smiled and gradually a comfortable feeling swept over her.

Martha had a bounce to her steps as she walked from the hospital to the Avenue a few blocks away. There she took the trolley home. She couldn't wait to share her experience with her family.

Round Corners

Chapter Twenty-seven

Second class midshipman, Mortimer Spooner Weigand, met classmate Richard Cuthbert on the tennis courts. They paired up for a doubles match. Mortimer quickly learned that Richard – not Dick – had excellent reflexes at the net. Not only did he have speed to reach for a ball but his wrist could redirect the return shot in the same movement. Mort was impressed. Mort preferred the back court play. Over the years at the prep school in New Hampshire, he had developed a hard, low level shot deep into the opponent's side of the court. Mort's strong and steady backhand had been his stroke to many victories.

After the game as they walked back together to Bancroft Hall, the dormitory that housed all midshipmen, they agreed to meet later. On Saturdays as members of the second class they were at liberty to exit the Yard and in civilian clothes wander around Annapolis.

When they met outside their dormitory, Richard asked, "Do you mind going for a ride? I know a nice little coffee shop on the outskirts of town." Mort was impressed that Richard had a vehicle. Second class midshipman were allowed to drive their own cars but not allowed to park them on campus. That privilege only started in the fourth year.

The guard stood at attention as they exited the United States Naval Academy. Richard led Mort to a parking lot a few blocks away from the base. They approached a vehicle covered with a gray canopy. "Grab one side," instructed Richard. "We'll fold this up and put it in the boot of the car." A fancy no top sports car stood before them. "Jump in," invited Richard. And jumping in is exactly what Mort had to do for the auto had no doors. "What make of car is this?" inquired

Mort. "It's a Bentley. My folks gave it to me when I graduated from Phillips Academy in Andover, MA."

Richard drove the Bentley through the quaint town of Annapolis, Maryland with its small colonial era brick buildings. They drove up Chesapeake Bay to a small village overlooking the bay and stopped at the "Blue and Gold". Richard commented, "The sandwiches here are large and delicious." Both men placed their order with Richard selecting lemonade and Mort choosing iced tea.

After hearty exchanges about the tennis match where they easily beat the "firsties" in three straight sets, Mort inquired, "Who appointed you to the Academy?" Richard answered, "Even though I went to school in Massachusetts, my family lives and has a long history in Newport, Rhode Island. My grandfather who passed away last year was a retired Captain in the Navy. Peter Gerry, our senator from Rhode Island, appointed me. My father had attended Harvard University with "uncle" Peter. After law school they both were admitted to the Rhode Island bar. My father joined a law firm in New York City where we have an apartment overlooking Central Park, but we all call Newport home. "Uncle" Peter drifted into politics. My father and "uncle" Peter are great friends."

Richard continued, "Uncle" Peter was born in New York City and still visits his family there regularly. Every visit is an opportunity for my father and him to get together and renew old times. "Uncle" Gerry has a very interesting history. His great grandfather was Vice President and has the dubious distinction of giving his surname, Gerry, to the term gerrymandering. He's a very influential man. After his divorce from a wealthy Washington society woman who I don't remember, he married my "auntie" Edith who is the widow of one of the Vanderbilts."

Richard inquired, "How did you get your appointment?" One of our Representatives, Edith Nourse appointed me. You may have heard of her. When her husband died, she ran in a special election as a Republican candidate and easily beat the former governor of our State in a landslide. Her husband served as congressman during World War I and Mrs. Nourse volunteered with the American Red Cross and with the Walter Reed Army Medical Center. Because of her stance on veteran issues, she's a favorite of the American Legion.

My mother and she attended the same private boarding school for girls in Lowell, MA. After graduation my mother was heartbroken when her friend announced that she going off to Madame Julien's, a finishing school in Paris, France. When Mrs. Nourse returned from France they renewed their friendship. My mother would visit her at their family home in Saco, Maine. I first met Mrs. Nourse when she started visiting our summer home in Saratoga Springs, New York. She loved to get away from the heat of D.C. and the intrigue of politics. Most summers she would spend two weeks with us. My mother would just love it. She had a companion for her visits to the spa and baths. They would reminisce and I was intrigued by her stories of her experiences in Europe. She is a delightful woman. She always wears a flower on her shoulder – either a gardenia or an orchid."

As they were replacing the gray canopy on the Bentley before re-entering the Yard, Mort asked, "Richard, would you like to play a game of singles tomorrow?" "I would love to," answered Richard.

On the tennis courts the next day Mort soon discovered that he and Richard were well matched even though their style of play was very different. What Richard had in agility, speed and quick reflexes, Mort offset it by strength and endurance. Mort had been taught by his coaches to play steady and hard. As in doubles his strength was in the back court. One of his coaches had suggested that after a missed first serve that he follow up with an equally hard serve. He had grown in confidence with this tactic and it took an opponent time to adjust to this uncommon strategy. It was quickly evident that Richard loved to bring his opponent to the net by a slice or drop ball where his quick reflexes put him into an advantage. Mort finally won their first match of singles together by sheer endurance. One of Mort's strategies was to play the first set steadily and with hard returns. In the second set he would pick up the pace and added more zip to his returns. Because of his great conditioning, he was even able to bring it up a notch on the third set. Mort who had been sickly in his youth had developed his body into a well-oiled machine.

Richard commented as they shook hands after the match, "You play a great game, Mort. I gave you everything I had but you wore me down. When I won the first set and learned some of your tactics and quirks, I thought I had you. You proved me wrong. What about a game tomorrow?"

For the rest of the year, Richard and Mort played a singles match of tennis almost daily. The consistency of play built up Richard's endurance while Mort improved his play at the net. It was a great rivalry.

Round Corners

Chapter Twenty-eight

In July of 1940, First class midshipman Mortimer was travelling with Richard Cuthbert in the fancy Bentley sports car. Richard was driving home to Newport, Rhode Island and offered to give Mort a ride to New Bedford. Both had successfully completed their first three years at the Naval Academy. Richard had been chosen as brigade commander. This was an honor reserved for a midshipman who had exhibited outstanding leadership performance. He was responsible for the brigade's day-to-day activities as well as the professional training of midshipmen. He was under the command of the active-duty Navy Captain. "I'm sorry that my grandfather, the old Navy captain, didn't have a chance to see me achieve this rank," Richard had commented when he was elevated to this position. "He would have been very proud. He was a real old salt."

Mort's wavy black hair blew back in the wind as they drove out of the Yard in Annapolis. Richard had now been assigned a parking space on campus. He was progressing rapidly in becoming prematurely bald. It gave him a look of distinction among the other midshipmen, but it required that he wear a cap as he drove his convertible.

They drove up the New Jersey Turnpike and as they approached New York City, Richard suggested, "Let's spend a night in the city. We could take in a Broadway play or go to a club. We could stay over at my dad's apartment. He's in Newport with the family this month. It seems the business of law slows down in the summer months." Richard was an intelligent, determined young man but also had a capacity for fun and relaxation.

Mort's initial internal reaction was one of reluctance. He was basically a shy guy and often felt awkward in new situations. In his early youth he had been a loner, but with his exposure to boarding school and at the Naval Academy he had developed a pleasant personality and increasing self-confidence. "Sure," agreed Mort. "I've only visited New York City twice and that's many years ago before my mother and father got divorced. My father owns and operates a clothing factory in the garment section of the city. My mother and I came to New York City together and even though my father wanted to show me the 'sights', she limited our tours to museums, the Statue of Liberty and Central Park."

It was close to 4 o'clock before they reached the entrance of the St. Regis Hotel where the Cuthbert's had a three bedroom apartment on the sixteenth floor overlooking Central Park. Mort was impressed by the French Beaux-Arts style lobby. The concierge recognized Richard and welcomed him, "Good afternoon, Master Cuthbert. I understand congratulations are in order. Your father was beaming with pride informing us of your new rank as brigade commander." "And who is this young man?" he continued.

Richard answered, "This is my classmate Mortimer Weigand. He's from the textile city of New Bedford, Massachusetts. I've just learned that his father has a shop here in the garment section of the city. We are travelling home and thought we would spend a night in the city." "Anything exciting happening in town?" asked Richard.

"I know you like jazz," commented the concierge. "Mezz Mezzrow who plays the clarinet and saxophone is at Jimmy Ryan's on 52nd. Sidney Bechet has teamed up with him. The trumpeter Oran 'Hot Lips' Page has joined them on a few occasions for some jam sessions. I've been told that those jam sessions have lasted way past the rising of the sun. When Mezz was arrested last year entering a club at the New York Worlds' Fair, he had sixty joints of marijuana on him. Even though he's white, he has declared himself a "voluntary negro". When he was sent to jail, he insisted that he was black and got himself transferred to the segregated prison's black section."

"What do you think?" asked Richard as he glanced at Mort. "It's a far cry from a museum and I think I'm ready to see another side of New York City," answered Mort.

After cleaning up in the apartment, Richard and Mort dressed in their Summer Whites uniforms. Around seven they descended by elevator to the lobby area. The concierge had placed a dinner reservation for them. Richard took the opportunity to introduce Mort to the new King Cole Bar adjacent to the dining room of the St. Regis. He explained, "That painting of Old King Cole was originally in Astor's now defunct Knickerbocker Hotel. Let me introduce you to our bartender, Fernand Petiot. He invented a drink which he calls the Red Snapper. Most people around the world are referring to it as the Bloody Mary."

Both men had refrained from drinking alcoholic beverages during their days at the Naval Academy. They both adhered to the academy's Honor Concept that frowned on the use of alcohol. Plus both men were committed to the care of their young bodies which had led them to compete daily at tennis. Fernand prepared them a non-alcoholic Bloody Mary. "You will experience the taste of the drink without the kick," said Fernand.

Over dinner Richard talked about other New York nightclubs. "I like the traditional style jazz played at Nick's in Greenwich Village. Eddie Condon who is a jazz banjoist and guitarist is a regular. The sophisticated variation on Dixieland music, that Condon and associates like Bobby Hackett with his cornet play at Nick's, is being nicknamed "Nicksieland. If we had more time we could travel to the Village but it sounds like an evening at Jimmy Ryan's will keep us up 'til the wee hours, especially if they start jamming."

The concierge had informed Richard that the Davidsons were in town. Richard had called their room at the Regis and learned that their daughter, Allison who had accompanied them to the city had gone on a shopping spree with her friend, Darlene. He informed Mr. Davidson, "A friend and I are staying overnight and I was wondering if Allison and her friend would be interested in joining us in going to a club. I know it's very late notice but we just arrived in town this afternoon. We are planning to leave no earlier than nine. Allison can reach us either in the apartment or in the restaurant. We have a reservation for seven." "I will give her the message," said Mr. Davidson.

As Richard and Mort were starting the house salad, that included fennel, thinly sliced prosciutto and pomegranate seeds on arugula lettuce, the maître d' came to their table with a telephone. Mort easily recognized that Richard's friend was responding to his invitation and seeing a growing flush on his cheeks correctly assumed that the invitation was accepted. Richard announced, "Allison and Darlene will be joining us. They just got back from shopping but will freshen up for the evening and will meet us in the lobby by 9:30." "This is great," said Richard as he rubbed his hands together in excitement. "I've only met her friend, Darlene, once or twice and never on a date. She is very pleasant and quite the looker. And if she's a friend of Allison, she has already made the grade."

The evening at Jimmy Ryan's exposed Mort to a whole new world. The jazz musicians were in their element with Mezz and Bechet playing off each other with a rhythm that defied the possible height and speed of each note. Darlene was in fact a beautiful woman. She sat close to him so that he could smell her delicate perfume that encircled him. They were close enough to hear each other but she didn't intrude on his space. As the evening progressed and the music rose in intensity, both couples just naturally had to get closer to make any brief comment. One time Mort had come close to Darlene to exclaim a few words of amazement about the music. He looked into the most beautiful clear blue eyes he had ever seen.

On the way back to the St. Regis, all four squeezed into the back seat of the cab. No one wanted to break the spell of intimacy that they had experienced together by someone going into the front passenger seat, as they had earlier when they travelled to the club. In the lobby the young women broke away reluctantly but with dignity.

The next day Richard dropped off Mort at the New Bedford Hotel near the Post Office of the city. Mort had rented a room there since his mother had given up the family home on County Street. Later he took a cab to neighboring Fairhaven to visit his mother. He had so much to tell her. It had taken him such a long time to get to this feeling of security and joy in his life. His mother had been very patient, loving and supportive. He hoped that she was doing well in her new living arrangements. Her letters were always upbeat and she never complained. He needed to reassure himself by this visit with her and hopefully receive a candid assessment from Mrs. Moriarity.

Round Corners

Book Five

Round Corners

Book Five

Chapter Twenty-nine

The Lepage family:

When Jean Paul and Claude entered their first floor tenement, a sense of excitement filled the room. Their sister, Martha, had arrived home a half-hour earlier. She was a first year nursing student at the local St. Luke's Hospital. She lived at the White Home located adjacent to the hospital. This was one of her few weekend breaks.

Mrs. Lepage looked up from the intense conversation she was having with Martha. One question was always leading to another, as she wanted to know everything that was happening in her daughter's life.

"Oh, Claude," she exclaimed with excitement, "you're home also. Are you staying for the weekend?" "Yes," answered Claude, "I have to be back in Quonset by Monday morning."

"Come sit with us," Mrs. Lepage said as she pointed to Martha who was sitting on the couch across from her. "We have so much to share. You too, Jean Paul. This is overwhelming. We'll have to have a good old-fashioned Sunday dinner with as many of the family as possible. I'm quite sure we can persuade your oldest sister Claudia and her new husband Paul to join us. They are still in the honeymoon phase and only have eyes for each other but a good family meal should provide an incentive."

"But here I go planning tomorrow and there is so much I want to know about your lives right now," said Mrs. Lepage as she redirected her thoughts. Jean Paul sat next to his sister on the couch and Claude took a chair next to his mother and soon all had their heads close together in a circle not wanting to miss a word.

"Martha was just telling me of her experiences at St. Luke's Hospital," started their mother. "There are now twenty-eight of us in the freshmen class," added Martha. "So far the class material, especially science and math, are challenging but our time on the floor of the hospital following the nurses in their routines helps to make it real."

"I especially like the pediatric section," Martha continued. "The little ones are sometimes so delicate and weak but the way they fight for life is a real marvel. Another area of hospital care that intrigues me is the emergency section where people with all kinds of injuries come for help. I find the pace frantic but the doctors and nurses show such great skills with lots of empathy for the patient."

Martha looked up to Claude; "Do you mind if I go upstairs to see Janet and her baby, Louise. I've been so looking forward to seeing how much Louise has grown since I last saw her. I promise to ask you a thousand questions when I come back down."

Martha squeezed by Jean Paul and turned back to him and gave him a big hug, "I miss you so much little brother." And off she ran out the door and skipped up to the third floor apartment. She could feel all the energy she had had as a young schoolgirl.

Mrs. Lepage turned her attention to Claude, "Now before you run off to your friends, tell me about your self and your work." Claude told her that he was fine and that he had put on a few pounds. They provide us good food at the mess hall and we work hard. Plus a few of us exercise a lot. We are trying to follow some of the strength and training regimens the enlisted are required to do each day. The extra pounds are all muscle." Claude flexed his right arm muscle for his mother and his brother, Jean Paul, to admire.

"I was telling Jean Paul and the people we met at the Labonte pharmacy that we are at the final phases of development of a military housing building. The engineers are putting it to its final paces this weekend. If all goes as anticipated we would be starting mass production soon. These are moveable structures and are especially designed for use on the Pacific Islands." Claude decided to keep his thoughts about joining the Navy to himself for now. He wanted his mother to bask in the sunny happiness of having her family around her. Plus he was aware that the unusually quiet Jean Paul who sat on the couch held a sad experience within him.

Claude opened the conversation, "Ma, Jean Paul experienced something frightening today at his work." Claude pointed to Jean Paul to continue. Rubbing his dark curly hair with both hands, Jean Paul who hardly ever sat quietly and only talked in quick passing sentences as he moved from one thing to another started, "We found the body of little baby behind a bathroom wall. It was just a dry skeleton."

Mrs. Lepage jumped from her chair and pulled Jean Paul into her warm, embracing arms. "Oh, my poor boy!" After a few quiet moments, Mrs. Lepage sat next to her son on the couch. "What's going to happen?" she asked. "The police are investigating. All those who found the body had our fingerprints taken at the downtown police station. They say that this is a new technique recently developed to help in discovering who may have done this …" Jean Paul couldn't say anymore.

Round Corners

Chapter Thirty

Janet jumped with joy as she opened the door to welcome an unexpected visitor. "Martha, what are you doing here? Are you, ok? We haven't seen you in months."

Martha hugged her sister-in-law; "I'm on a weekend break. I'm just fine. Where is Louise?"

"She's sleeping right now but should awaken soon. She seems to have developed a schedule of waking from her nap just about the time her sister, Charlotte, comes running up the stairs from school. It may be from all the noise that she makes upon opening the door and telling me all the excitement of her day," answered Janet.

Martha and Janet had grown very close after the birth of Louise a few years earlier. Janet had given birth to a slender, somewhat fragile blond haired girl. The first year, Louise thrived under the loving care of Janet and Al. She was also a favorite of her young aunts who lived on the first floor.

Soon after her first super-grand birthday party, Louise developed some flu-like symptoms. Louise's happy, gurgling smiles slowly receded. She would lie there in her crib or in someone's arms quite fatigued. She would quickly run a fever and cried while she seemingly pointed to her head. Along with these occasional headaches, her throat would be sore and red.

Martha would spend hours upstairs with Janet, holding and comforting the baby. Ben Labonte, the druggist, had prescribed some comforting measures but when these provided only temporary relief, he recommended that Doctor Peter Rosen, a pediatrician, see Louise. Martha had gone with Al and Janet to the doctor's appointment.

Janet told Martha, "Louise is back to her old self. She's been putting on weight and just loves to exercise with her father."

"I'm so happy," answered Martha. "My interest in nursing started with my contact with Doctor Rosen. I was so impressed by the way he used those sensitive and professional hands to examine Louise. He was the one who ordered cultures to be taken of Louise's stools and throat swabs."

"We were so devastated when he told us that Louise had contracted a polio virus," stated Janet. "He tried to reassure us that it was discovered at a very early stage. And that even though there was no cure for the virus, there was a very slight chance that Louise would develop the more serious symptoms like respiratory problems and paralysis. You were so helpful, Martha, in keeping up our spirits. You just knew that everything would be fine."

Martha smiled shyly, "I think it was Doctor Rosen who gave me that confidence. The one thing that he impressed upon me was that the virus was very infectious. We needed to be very careful with her feces, "poops" as I used to call it before learning a new word in nursing school, as well as mucus or phlegm. We could protect Louise from being further infected and keep it from spreading to other members of the family."

"I've learned that President Franklin Roosevelt has been so helpful in increasing scientific research," stated Martha. "Did you know that he contracted paralytic polio in the early 1920's? However, he tries to hide it from the public. When he came to New Bedford a few years ago to deliver a campaign speech with Eleanor at his side, he was seen and photographed mostly in his car waving to the people. Did you know that he went to the Delano Homestead in Fairhaven for a lunch with his mother who had secretly traveled from New York?"

"No," answered Janet. "You are becoming so educated and knowledgeable of so many things. We did learn recently that the

President was instrumental in starting the March of Dimes campaign to fight infantile paralysis. Al tries to get donations from his customers to help the cause. Most know about Louise's brush with polio and give as generously as they can in these difficult times."

Janet led Martha to Louise's room. "You've been very patient, Martha," said Janet, "let's go see Louise." Louise began to stir in her bed. She was almost three years old and had grown so much since Martha had last seen her. Louise opened her eyes and slowly recognized Martha standing by her mother's side. "Mart . . ," she cried out in surprise and joy. Louise stood up on her bed and gave Martha many hugs and kisses. Martha discovered that Louise's diaper was wet. "May I change her," asked Martha, "I've missed these special times."

Janet opened the shades and pointed to a changing table near the bed. "Enjoy yourselves. I've got some laundry to take in that's hanging on the line. When you're finished with Louise, I have a secret to share with you." Janet went to her third floor hallway and opened the window. She started to remove the many diapers and other clothing from the clothes line that crossed the yard to a pole. From her vantage point she could see the numerous clothes lines with clothes flapping in the drying wind that dotted the neighborhood. The clothes pins were removed and placed in a cloth sack that hung on the wall near the window.

A little later Janet shared with Martha that she had recently discovered that she was pregnant. "Oh, I'm so happy for you and my brother, Al."

"No one else in both families knows of this yet. I only knew for sure a few days ago and just told Al the news," continued Janet. "After Louise's illness we were both afraid and reluctant to have another child, but since Louise is doing so well, we tried again and it worked real fast."

110

Round Corners

Chapter Thirty-one

On Sunday afternoon the Lepage family gathered for a traditional family meal. Everyone was present and it required that two tables had to be set up to accommodate a gathering of sixteen. Janet sat with her two daughters, Charlotte and Louise, at the smaller table with Martha. Someone had suggested that the two youngest Lepages join that table seating arrangement but young Ronald would have nothing to do with joining a group of all girls, so eleven gathered at the dinner table set up in the front parlor.

Claude introduced Anne to the family. "Some of you know Anne. She lives in the six-family across the street. Ma agreed that I could invite her over to join us for dinner." Anne blushed as the family members greeted her warmly and noisily. The older girls helped Mrs. Lepage bring the heaping bowls and platters of food from the kitchen to the table. Charlotte, the eldest granddaughter, had climbed onto her Pepere's lap at the head of the table. When it was his time to cut the ham into slices, Janet retrieved Charlotte, but not without some resistance. Memere had prepared a boiled dinner which along with the ham included fresh cabbage, carrots and potatoes – all boiled together. It was a mushy meal but the Lepages loved it.

Paul LaMontagne who had recently married the oldest of the Lepage girls, Claudia, participated but it was evident that this meal was not his favorite. Paul told the group, "I just got a job as a carpenter at Fort Rodman. The army is building a number of wooden barracks to replace the tents that presently houses the 27th National Guard Regiment. Both the National Guard and regular Army Coast Artillery units are being activated and brought up to full strength. I've seen plans that include the building of a new mess hall, a chapel, bachelor officers' quarters, a post exchange where the enlisted men as well as those working on the base will be able to purchase items at reduced prices. I'm looking forward to buying my cigarettes there. The master plan includes a paymaster's office built with a large wall-in safe, a new hospital with operating theaters and a fire station. Quite the project! It should provide me steady employment for a couple of years."

Claudia who sat next to Paul looked up at him just beaming with pride. She had recently obtained a secretarial position at the Aerovox Corp. She was a recent graduate of the Kinyon-Campbell secretarial school. A few years earlier, the Aerovox had moved its plant and offices along the upper reaches of the Acushnet River. Located on Belleville Avenue, it was only a few blocks away from the Lepage residence. The company was a major manufacturer of condensers, capacitors and other electrical components. Cornell Dubilier Co. in the south end of New Bedford was its competitor. They were often in court claiming that one or the other had infringed on their respective patents.

Claude thought that his brother-in-law's reference to the military buildup at Fort Rodman was a good introduction to his announcing his intentions of joining the Navy. As he stood up to reach for the bowl of boiled potatoes, Claude interjected, "We have just completed building a proto-type of a corrugated metal structure called a Quonset Hut that will be prefabricated and shipped to the islands in the Pacific. Last year Rear Admiral Ben Morell was authorized to form a new naval construction battalion. It will be a unique organization within the Navy that will support the Navy and Marines in remote locations and defend themselves if attacked. Last night I informed Ma and Pa and Anne," as he grabbed and held her hand, "that I was planning to join this select group, when it is up and running. That's if they will have me. This battalion is being built with experienced and highly skilled craftsmen…electricians, carpenters, equipment operators. I figure that since I worked on the development of the portable housing that I have a good chance of being selected to be part of this exclusive group in the Navy."

Al, Claude's older brother remarked, "That's a dangerous area of the world right now, Claude. What I'm hearing from my customers on the bread route is that Japan is expanding its empire to many of the islands in the Pacific Ocean. I'm told that they are well-trained and determined to take over that part of the world, including even China and India. Are you sure you want to put yourself into such danger?"

Claude answered, "What I'm hearing at work is that the country is on the verge of initiating a draft. And I'd rather select my area of military operations than have it imposed upon me. The prospects in Europe are terrifying. Adolf Hitler is proving to be a satanic dictator as he expands his domination of his European neighbors."

Mr. Lepage hit his water glass with his utensil, "Enough of this kind of talk. We will frighten the children. Ma, what's for dessert?"

"I baked two nice apple pies this morning which I'm sure most of you smelled as you came into the house earlier," answered Mrs. Lepage.

Paul who was known to the family as a fun loving guy always with an exciting adventure, picked up his father-in-law's clue and suggested, "Who's for going to the Orpheum Theater later this evening? The vaudeville show that was supposed to end last week has been held over by popular demand."

Martha spoke up, "Janet, why don't you and Al go to the show. I'll take care of the girls. It will be a treat for me."

As Janet was about to turn down the invitation, little Charlotte spoke up, "Yes, please go and have fun. Being with Martha will be our treat."

Claude and Anne agreed to join the group. "I'm sure I can convince your folks," said Claude to Anne.

Al looked over at Janet. She knew what he was thinking. "I have to get up early tomorrow morning. I'm usually in bed by eight on Sunday night." But as he looked at Paul, he knew that he would not be easily convinced. Paul somehow always managed to get him out of his customary routines."

Paul picked up the vibe and stated, "We all have to work tomorrow. And from my vantage point a fun time together is sometimes more refreshing than a long night sleep."

So the three young couples were off to the theater. The show started at six. Paul, the leader of the group, was able to get second row seats in the balcony. The vaudeville shows consisted of a comedian, who was also the announcer, a few gymnast and acrobats performing feats of unbelievable dexterity, and of course a group of scantily clad dancing-girls. The highlight of this show was the comedian who was midget size and who could tell a tale that brought the house down with laughter. Janet found herself laughing hysterically. She had not laughed so outrageously in her life. The group around her found her laughter infectious so that rows in front and behind them were bursting in painful joy and trying hard to catch their breath.

Toward the end of the show, three tall girls came on stage prancing and moving to the music concealed by long feathery wings. The men in the audience were trying to glimpse the beautiful bodies behind the slithering motions of the wings. As they left the stage the last girl in the line casually dropped her wings and disappeared behind the curtains. Some in the audience whistled expressing their appreciation.

Round Corners

Book Six

Round Corners

Book Six

Chapter Thirty-two

Calling the young to battle:

Martha Lepage and Barbara O'Toole completed their training in nursing at St. Luke's Hospital in May, 1942. Neither one had missed a day of their education in their three years at the White Home. As roommates during those years they had encouraged and supported each other to carry on even when one or the other did not feel well or up to a particular challenge in their training. Barbara had found the training in psychiatric nursing especially difficult.

St. Luke's Hospital had an affiliation with Taunton State Psychiatric Hospital. All nursing students spent three months on the Taunton State Hospital campus. Some of the patients frightened her and conditions at the hospital were terrible. The treatment they were taught to administer consisted of tub baths, restraint and isolation. All seemed so archaic and medieval. Their caring of patients who returned to the wards after shock therapy made Barbara sick to her stomach. They returned in a vegetative state and needed to be assisted in bathing, eating and other daily chores. True, their alarming and dangerous behavior had been arrested but at what cost.

Martha who had been more exposed to some of the disquieting elements of life handled this part of the training with composure. When Barbara threatened to leave the program, Martha counseled her to take it one day at a time. She pointed out the patients who had been calmed by Barbara's gentle and solicitous care for them. Plus Martha would remind her, "This is only three months in our training.

And you have already learned that you won't be choosing this area of nursing as your specialty."

Barbara had received excellent preparation in high school in mathematics and sciences. St. Anthony's High School that Martha attended emphasized the humanities. When Martha thought she would never comprehend a particular area of study, Barbara would patiently assist her to step through the elements of the problem. They were good roommates but also great study companions.

When President Roosevelt declared war on Japan after the attack on Pearl Harbor, both young women decided to enlist in the Navy. After successfully passing the State Board exam and becoming official Registered Nurses, they filled out application papers for the Navy Nurse Corp. They were first sent to the Chelsea Naval Hospital for a physical exam. A few weeks later both received written orders to report to the Newport, Rhode Island Naval Hospital for training. There they were outfitted in nurse uniforms and became acquainted with Navy lingo. They were also introduced to marching.

The Newport Naval Hospital cared for sick sailors and their dependents who were assigned to the base. Trained hospital corpsman under the supervision of a female nurse cared for the male population. The wards, in contrast to St. Luke's Hospital, were very large with as many as twenty patients. There were a few private rooms at the entrance of each ward for the more seriously ill. Naval officers had their own special ward in a wing separated from the enlisted men.

After a six month training at the hospital, Martha received correspondence in a sealed, registered Navy envelope. "I'm afraid to open it," exclaimed Martha. "It must contain my next assignment. Maybe I should wait until you receive your orders before I open mine."

Barbara advised her to open her letter, "What I've heard from others, the Navy only gives us a few days before reporting to a new assignment."

Martha's hands were shaking when she opened the envelope. She read it quickly, "I'm going to the Naval Hospital in Oakland, California. I have to report there by December 29th. That's ten days from now. Oh my God, Barbara, do you think you'll receive a different assignment? I don't know what I would do without you at my side."

Barbara courageously answered, "Let's not worry about that now. You have to get your affairs in order. Luckily, you'll be able to spend a few days with your family at Christmas. I know how close you are to them. Who knows, my orders may be in tomorrow's mail."

Sure enough Barbara received her registered letter the following day. Martha crossed her fingers as Barbara opened her letter. As she read it to herself, Martha observed sadness in Barbara's eyes. Bravely she told Martha, "I'm being assigned to a U. S. Naval dispensary in Miami, Florida. I'm to report on December 27th."

Both looked at each other in shock. "We'll keep in contact," suggested Martha trying to be brave. Barbara added, "We never had any assurance that we would get the same assignment. We have some great and important work to do for our service men and their families."

They hugged each other and cried. The almost four years they had been together were extremely special. Martha commented, "We're really in the Navy now."

Two days after Christmas, Martha was being driven to the Naval Air Facility at Camp Edwards. She had been assigned a seat aboard a Lockheed P-38 Lightning that was returning to Burbank's Union Airport on the West Coast. Janet sat in the front seat with Al in his grey panel delivery truck. Martha sat with Al and Janet's daughters Charlotte and Louise on make shift seats in the rear of the truck. The young girls and Martha had often ridden in this fashion to many activities and events. They just loved it. It seemed to be a fitting way to send Martha off on her way.

Round Corners

Chapter Thirty-three

When Claude Lepage came home from Quonset Point, Rhode Island a few days before Christmas the mood in the household was one of fear. A few days earlier everyone had become aware that Japan had attacked the naval fleet at Pearl Harbor. News reels in the movie theaters showed the USS Arizona sinking into the bay after burning for two days. On December 8, 1941 the United States had declared war on Japan.

Up to that point the war in Europe seemed distant. The United States involvement had been extremely limited. When the U.S. Neutrality Act was passed late in the year of 1939 allowing the French and British to buy arms and only on a strictly cash basis, American isolationists had declared the act "an outrage." When the presence of German U-boats on the East Coast started to endanger the cargo shipping lanes, lights along the coastline were ordered to be darkened including the covering of windows in private homes. This single act brought the potential horror of war into the consciousness of ordinary United States citizens.

No longer could they avoid the growing disturbances abroad, including the invasion of Belgium, France, Poland and the Netherlands. When the Luftwaffe began the bombing of England and Paris, President Franklin Delano Roosevelt asked Congress for huge increases in military preparations. A few months later the Selective Training and Service Act introduced the first peacetime conscription in the United States history for men between 21 and 35 years of age. The United States became more deeply involved in the European and Pacific conflicts when President Roosevelt signed the Lend Lease Act which was passed by the full Congress that allowed Britain, China, and other allied nations to purchase military equipment and to defer payment until after the war.

120

Claude Lepage announced that, like his sister Martha, he had been accepted into the Navy and that he was being sent for basic training at Camp Peary in Virginia. The news was received with silence as each of the family members tried to grasp the reality of Claude's decision. "Now, don't cry," Claude stated as he saw tears flooding the eyes of his mother and sisters. "Camp Peary is a Seabee training base. We'll be learning new skills that will help us when we are assigned. After basic training, I'll be returning home. You'll be seeing me in no time."

Later that afternoon Claude went across the street to see Anne. He had decided that it would be best to break the news to her slowly. "Oh, Claude, you're home!" Anne said as she welcomed him to the Saulnier second floor tenement. She grabbed his hand and brought him into the living room to meet her parents. She was thrilled when Claude held her around the waist as they proceeded together into the room. Mr. Saulnier commented, "It's so nice to see that you will be home for Christmas. Anne has been pacing around the house all day and constantly peeking through the curtains to see if you had arrived. It sounds from her excitement that you surprised her."

Claude agreed to join the Saulniers for dinner. Anne was an only child. This small family gathering was certainly going to be quite different for him. He asked, "Is it alright if we go out for a walk before dinner?" Anne's mother readily agreed, "We won't be eating for another two hours or so." Looking at her daughter, she cautioned, "Dress warmly and don't forget your scarf and mittens. It's turning cold." Louise reassured her mother but the heat and excitement that was passing through her body as Claude touched her hardly made the weather her concern."

Hand in hand Claude and Anne walked up the street to the Avenue. "Let's cross over to the park," suggested Claude. They strolled by the duck pond admiring the ducks and watched as some of the neighborhood children were testing the ice that was beginning to harden. One boy spoke out excitedly, "Looks like we may be able to use our ice skates over the vacation." One girl clasped her hand in prayer, "I'm hoping I get a new pair of white skates this Christmas. My old ones that my sister handed down to me squish my toes."

Claude and Anne found an empty bench near the warming house. Anne surprised Claude by asking, "Did you get accepted into the Seabees?" Feeling relieved that Anne had initiated the conversation of his enlistment in the Navy, Claude answered, "Yes. Yesterday, I got the word as well as two other co-workers."

"What happens, now?" inquired Anne. "The Monday after New Year's day we've been told to meet at the railroad station in Providence," answered Claude, "no later than six in the morning. About seven recruits will be boarding the train for New York's Pennsylvania Station. Another group will be joining us there for our trip to Camp Peary in Virginia. There we will be receiving basic training."

"This is all happening very quickly," stated Anne. "How long will you be gone? Will you write to me? Virginia seems so far away. You won't be dropping by on weekends."

Claude reassured her, "We were told that basic training will last about eight weeks. Of course, I'll write, every day." Suddenly Anne felt a chill as the reality of their separation was imminent.

Claude stood up and held out his hand, "Let's go get warmed up inside the church."

Anne could hear the music of Christmas chants coming from St. Joseph's Church. "That's a good idea," agreed Anne. "Along with getting warmer, let's also pray that God will watch over you and keep you safe. I'm missing you already." Claude and Anne were comforted by the familiar smell of the wax candles burning before the statue of Our Lady.

Paul LaMontagne had volunteered to take Claude to the railway station in Providence. He had recently purchased a used Crossley De Soto. He kept it well polished and shiny. This was his first major purchase. He had negotiated a price of $189.00 from the original owner who had lost his job at the Hathaway Mills and couldn't keep up with the payments.

The Saulniers had reluctantly agreed to allow their daughter Anne to accompany Claude to Providence. Anne was a senior at St. Anthony's High School. She and Claude had gone to see Soeur Marthe de Rome, the principal of the school. Although quite shy, Anne was well liked by her teachers and classmates and was a conscientious student. The principal readily agreed, "This is an important moment in your lives. Just be sure to come to school as soon as you return from Providence. Your friends and teachers will be here to cheer you up."

Around four in the morning of Claude's departure for military service, the entire Lepage clan was out in the cold morning air waving him good bye. His younger brothers were still in their pajamas wiping a mixture of sleep and tears from their eyes. Paul finally started the engine and pulled away from the wooden three deckers. To Claude's surprise a group of cousins who lived next door had gathered on their front porch and were also waving him along. One young boy stood at attention and saluted.

Paul and Claude sat in the front seat of the vehicle and Claude's oldest sister, Loretta, sat with Anne. They held hands. Anne looked out of the rear window and saw her parents holding each other as they stood on the second floor porch of their residence. Paul's wife needed to be at work at the Aerovox by seven while Loretta worked the second shift at the Acushnet Company. Paul's easy style kept a conversation going between him and Claude. The young women in the back seat were quiet.

A little after five thirty, Paul was driving up to the train station. Claude pointed out, "There's our group of recruits. The one in the white navy uniform was our recruiter and will accompany us to New York City. He's only a few years older than the rest of us who are joining."

Paul opened the trunk of the vehicle and Claude pulled out the duffel bag with his belongings. His brother Al and his wife Janet had purchased it for him as a going away gift. Al had been collecting extra change from the bread route in a glass jar in the pantry just next to the place where he hung up the keys of his gray panel bread truck. After handshakes, embraces and a long kiss from Anne, Claude pulled the duffel bag onto his shoulders and approached the group of recruits. They were all smiles as they pointed out the red lipstick that covered Claude's cheeks and lips.

Round Corners

Chapter Thirty-four

The Navy recruiter who accompanied the young men from Providence escorted them from New York's Penn Station. When they reached the city streets Claude stood amazed at seeing the height of the buildings nearby and the rush of pedestrians on the broad sidewalks. There was a constant blaring of horns all around that gave the scene a sense of urgency.

The group was led to a bus idling a few blocks away. There two solemn looking naval officers directed them to stow their gear in an open area under the bus. "Quickly find an empty seat on the bus," ordered one officer. "We are ready to depart."

Claude found a seat toward the rear of the bus. He had anticipated that he would continue to travel with Tom Singleton. Tom and he had worked together on the assembling of the huts at Quonset Point. He had met him on the train from Providence and was surprised to know that he had also enlisted with the Seabees. However, there were no two seats next to each that were available.

Claude introduced himself to a stocky dark haired young man, "I'm Claude Lepage. We just came in from Providence." Claude was greeted with a firm handshake, "I'm Ralph Papaleo. My friends call me Grubby. I've been working as a heavy equipment mechanic or grease monkey on a construction project near Times Square. This is the cleanest I've been in years. Before leaving home my mother insisted that I get a good scrubbing. She is concerned that I won't make the grade of becoming a member of the Navy. She has a point. I don't know if I will ever be able to keep one those white navy outfits clean."

Claude noticed the distinctive accent and learned, "I'm from Brooklyn. It's a borough of New York. Most of us in the neighborhood are Italian. I'm going to miss the gang, especially the games of stickball we played on the weekend."

After a few hours on the road with hardly a break in their conversation, Ralph asked, "Did you bring anything to eat for the ride?" Claude had to admit that he had never thought of it. "My mother wouldn't let me leave without something for the road." From the inner pocket of his heavy jacket, Ralph pulled out something wrapped in brown paper. "Do you want to share in this salami sandwich?"

When Claude started to explain that he didn't want to deprive Ralph of his lunch, Ralph opened the other side of his jacket, "Don't you worry about that. There a lot more right there, plus what I stuffed into my outer pockets."

Claude was astonished when Ralph removed a bottle of Coke from one of his many pockets. He removed the bottle cap with one of the attachments of his knife and offered it to Claude. "Don't be shy. Take a slug. Just keep me some to wash down this sandwich. It's the only bottle I brought for the ride. I didn't expect that I would have a guest for lunch."

By the middle of the afternoon and after a nap, Ralph turned to Claude, "You can call me, Grubby. You have become my first friend in the Navy."

The sun was setting as the bus passed through the gates of Camp Peary. Once off the bus and with their personal gear next to them, the recruits were lined up by alphabetical order. Claude Lepage found that he was only two persons away from Ralph "Grubby" Papaleo. The young men were further divided into two groups. One of the officers who had accompanied the men on the bus took command of Claude's group. "There will be no talking when you are under my command. You are assigned to barrack number 12 which is to the west, that's where the sun is setting. You have five minutes to take your gear into the barracks and leave it at the end of one of the bunks and return here pronto."

When the men returned, they were lined up in formation – five men in a row and ten deep. "My name is Lieutenant McCloskey. You will always address me as, "Sir." Stand straight and tall. Remember the men next to you. Anytime you come to attention in front of me, this is the only formation I want to see."

"It is now chow time," announced McCloskey. The men started to relax and slouched. McCloskey barked out an order, "Attention. You are not dismissed. You will not be dismissed until you hit the sack. We will march over to the mess hall. You will walk straight and tall and remain in formation."

In the mess hall the recruits were instructed to take a tray and move down a line where food was placed on the tray. There were no exceptions. A piece of meat, that Claude thought he recognized as a slice of SPAM, large spoons of mashed potatoes and some green vegetables, two slices of bread and a tin cup of coffee were placed on the trays as the men moved along the row. The men were instructed, "Sit in your groups of five on the benches on one side of the table. Five tables have been assigned to this company for the duration of your stay at Peary. You have fifteen minutes to eat your meal. When finished I will call you to stand in formation outside the mess hall. Before you leave, stack your empty trays at the end of each table. Remember I said empty trays. They don't stack up well if not clean and empty."

The men ate in silence. Claude looked down his row to see if he could catch sight of Grubby. Right behind him, he heard Lieutenant McCloskey, "Look straight ahead, recruit. What's your name?" "Claude Lepage," he answered. Lieutenant McCloskey ordered, "Stand up, recruit. What's your name?" Claude suddenly remembered, "Claude Lepage, Sir!"

After chow the recruits were issued blue work uniforms. It consisted of two pairs of blue denim pants and a long sleeve and short sleeve lighter blue chambray shirt. There were three sizes – large, medium and small. These were handed out without measuring tape by a sailor whose keen eye sized up the men. If the pant legs were too long, the option was to roll them up and if too short a recruit sported high waters. The recruits were able to provide their hat size. The standard white "Dixie Cup" hat issued to each sailor was the pride of the enlisted man.

Before retiring for the night, the recruits were introduced to the latrine. And were informed that reveille the next morning was at five. The day started with the recruits drilling in formation for an hour and then doing push-ups, squats and dashes. At seven the recruits were marched to the mess hall.

After breakfast the recruits were marched to the firing range, there the Marines took over their training. Claude Lepage, Tom Singleton and eight other recruits received their instruction from a Captain John Peterson. "This weapon you are receiving is called a M1903 Springfield which is being mass produced by Remington Arms. It is a bolt action five cartridge clip loading shoulder weapon. It is capable of delivering 20 shots per minute of accurate fire. As a member of the Seabees, you are not only part of a construction battalion but will be called upon to provide protection for your units in the front lines of a mission. Knowledge of your weapon and its proper care could mean the difference of life or death."

"You'll notice that each stripper clip contains 5 cartridges and as standard issue you are receiving a cloth bandolier with an additional 12 clips. These clips now contain dummy cartridges for drill purposes. The primer does not contain any percussion composition. Our initial drill is to accustom you to the operation of loading the rifle. And as part of each day's exercise, you will be charged with the breakdown, cleaning and reassembling of your weapon. A dirty weapon is a danger to you and your buddies," emphasized the Marine Captain.

After midday chow the recruits received their Seabees assignments. Claude wasn't surprised to see that Grubby was assigned to the motor pool. However he was taken aback when he was called to join the pontoon construction group. He had anticipated that he would be assigned to the Quonsett Hut division.

The Navy had already learned that the islands in the far Pacific were largely inaccessible outposts. These places had no facilities for docking and handling of the supplies, necessary to equip the men and machines required for a military campaign. Temporary substitutes were being devised to overcome these deficiencies. The basic pontoon became an integral part of amphibious warfare.

Tom Singleton joined Claude's working group. "I'm surprised we weren't assigned to the Quonsett Hut division," echoed Tom. They soon discovered that their experience in constructing the huts helped them in the assignment of creating and installing pontoon piers and floating docks. Claude commented as they moved sections into the water, "It looks like we're going to get wet, today." Sure enough! Most of the day they stood in water waist high assembling a section of a pontoon pier.

Two weeks later Lieutenant McCloskey commended the pontoon division, "In just under twelve days, you have completed a pontoon pier. More importantly, a cargo vessel was able to draw alongside and successfully unload its cargo. Congratulations, men."

The eight weeks of basic training went by quickly. Claude tried to keep his promise to Anne of writing daily. Some nights he found he was too exhausted. However, when he received his first letter from Anne which had been sealed by a kiss of red lipstick, his energy perked up. His bunk mates teased him and he thought mostly out of jealousy. He was a happy young man and in love.

Round Corners

Chapter Thirty-five

One day Janet Lepage's younger brother, Robert Paradis, informed his mother and sister that he had been drafted into the Army. He had previously discussed this news with his father and older brother, Raphael, who owned the luncheonette on the Avenue.

Almost every Sunday Al would bring his wife Janet and now their two young daughters, Louise and Charlotte, to visit Janet's family. Sometime they joined the family for a Sunday meal or made a shorter visit after sharing in the traditional Sunday dinner with the Lepages. Al appreciated that Janet and her mother were very close to each other and that Mrs. Paradis missed her only daughter. Al and Janet lived in the third floor tenement where his parents and large group of siblings lived, so hardly a day or even an hour went by without him, Janet and the girls having some contact with a family member. He thought it was only fair to make an effort to visit his in-laws regularly.

Knowing that his mother and sister had already been fretful that this day would come, Robert shared this news in as a matter of fact way as possible. He explained how he had met with Army personnel and learned that he was going to Fort Devens about a three hour drive away. He told them, "Fort Devens has been designated a reception center for all the men in New England who will serve as one year draftees. I've been told that after a few months of basic training, I will be receiving leave time on weekends to come home."

The following Wednesday Robert was to report at Fort Devens. It was decided that his brother, Raphael, and Al Lepage would drive Robert to his destination. Both men rushed through their day. Raphael left the luncheonette soon after cooking the midday meal and Al made his last delivery of bread by one-thirty. Al picked up Janet and the baby and they drove quietly to the Paradis home where Raphael was changing his clothes for the trip. Janet had made arrangements with Clara, the oldest of Al's sisters, to meet Charlotte at St. Joseph's School at the end of her school day.

Mrs. Paradis was doing her best to keep her emotions from disturbing her youngest son, Robert, her baby, before leaving for what she was convinced was a worthy and patriotic moment in his life. As she hugged him, she whispered, "Tu est mon cher enfant. Que le Bon Dieu soit avec toi."

Janet and Mildred, Raphael's wife, couldn't withhold their tears. Robert did his best not to show his reluctance to have them kiss him with their wet cheeks. Raphael came to his rescue, "We need to get going. Robert has to report before dark." Al grabbed Robert's bag and put it into the trunk of Raphael's Chevrolet, "Let's be on our way."

Later that night as Robert lay fully awake on a hard bunk bed, he experienced a certain fear of the unknown. From the moment he had received his draft notice, all he had felt was an excitement of a new adventure and the sense that he had suddenly become a man. Now for the first time in his life, the unknown became frightening. He found himself reverting to something he had left behind in his growing up years. He prayed. He asked God to watch over all his family and friends and he mentioned each by name. And as he slowly fell asleep, he felt a growing assurance that things would be fine.

Very early the next morning Robert, along with thousands of young recruits in basic training throughout the country, was learning the discipline of marching in unison with others. This was followed by strenuous exercise that Robert had always enjoyed. He liked the feeling of being physically fit and the deep breathing and perspiration that it required.

Like so many of his new comrades, Robert learned to expand his knowledge of others and to appreciate the unique differences each possessed. At breakfast Robert met Larry Crowther and Curly Molloy. Larry had come from a paper mill town in Maine and Curly, with curly red hair and freckles on his cheeks, was from South Boston. Curly differed from Robert and Larry by his sophisticated city ways. "I don't know if I'm going to be able to adjust to all this fresh air and the quiet we had last night," stated Curly. "I miss the smell of the exhaust of the busses going down the street and the street vendors hawking their wares. On summer nights our neighborhoods didn't ever quiet down."

Robert was fascinated by Larry's accent and the slang words he used. When Robert had asked Larry where he had come from, Larry answered, "Ah-yuh, I'm from East Millinocket, way up in the lumber country of Maine. My family moved there from Bah Harbah when I was nine. My father works for the Great Northern Paper Company. Ah-yuh, when a new dam and a hydroelectric power station were built on the Penobscot River, the company recruited workers from all over the State. That's when my daddy took the family all the way up tah Millinocket for some work. The pulp and paper mill can produce tons of marketable paper each day. Large rolls of paper are transported to the large city newspaper companies from Boston to New York in a constant steady flow. My first job was aboard one of those rigs. I travelled as fah as Hartford, Connecticut one time."

Basic training lasted a total of ten weeks. Robert could have easily been a model for an Army recruiter's poster. With his fine head of wavy dark brown hair, this dressed Army soldier could turn any young woman's head. After basic training ended, the draftees learned that their projected time of remaining at Fort Devens had been shortened. Most of the 45th Infantry Division to which Robert belonged had received basic combat training as well as amphibious assault training in preparation for an invasion of Italy. On June 8, 1943 the division sailed for the Mediterranean region combat loaded. However, Robert and Larry Crowther were sent to El Paso, Texas. Overland transport of troops and materiel was anticipated once the Allied forces secured beach heads in Europe.

Round Corners

Chapter Thirty-Six

Because Robert Paradis had previous training and experience as an auto mechanic, he and Larry Crowther, who had driven heavy rigs hauling trees out of the woods of Maine, were chosen with about two hundred others for training in the driving and maintenance of army trucks. In El Paso, Robert and Larry belonged to an all-white trucking unit. For the first time in his young life, Robert was exposed to other transportation companies that consisted of all black men. He learned that combat units were not integrated.

Larry treated his new 2 ½ ton six-wheel drive General Motors truck as his baby. Robert and he were lucky to team up together. Under Robert's guidance, the two men pored over the instruction manuals. Robert pointed out, "The more we are familiar with our equipment, the better we will be able to survive in the war zone."

They spent hours under the hood of the truck, first one side flipping the side over the top and then the other. "This is how you clean a carburetor," instructed Robert. This job became routine. Driving through the dry sandy soil of El Paso, it took constant maintenance to keep their "deuce-and-a-half" in top running order. This was a nickname given to the versatile truck. Each day the trucks came under inspection by a commanding officer. Robert suggested a competition with Larry, "Let's see how long it takes us to change a tire. One time you'll be in the lead and I'll assist and then vice-versa. We'll time ourselves." For the next few weeks, they engaged in this competition on their own time."

One day as Larry drove and bounced through the rough terrain on a delivery mission to a neighboring field office; a chain fell from the truck and was dragged along in the sand. When they attached it firmly to the hooks on the front bumper, the chain shined in the sunlight. At inspection, the squad leader commented favorably on the condition and look of their well-polished truck and shiny chain. Larry glanced at Robert and stated, "Isn't that a hum-dingah! You be sure that we'll be draggin' this chain in the sands before our next inspection."

That weekend the transport company was given leave privileges into El Paso. Larry asked Robert and a few of the men they associated with in the barracks, "Do yah want to go to the USO dance Saddee night?" All agreed. A bus was scheduled to leave for El Paso, soon after chow. Larry was waiting impatiently for Robert, "Ain't you ready yet? It's prettineah time to go!"

Robert and Larry were reluctant to return to their lonely barracks. After meeting and dancing with different girls, both had a special one latched onto them before the last dance. They got to exchange names and promised to be looking for each other at the next dance.

Over the Christmas holidays the men were given leave to go home for ten days. They had gotten instructions to report to Fort Pickett in Virginia for their final training. They were told to expect to ship out to the UK soon thereafter. The transportation company met up with other sections of the 45th Infantry Division. One day Larry excitedly ran up to Robert, "I just bumped inta Curly. When most of the men shipped out to the Mediterranean six months back, he was kept here with others so that they could train on a new anti-aircraft piece. They're shipping out by the end of the week to assist in the defense of London. He's in numba 89 barracks. I told him we would meet him there after chow."

It was a great re-union. Stories and laughs were shared and Curly informed them, "I just got engaged to my high school sweetheart, Meagan. If I wasn't leaving so soon, we probably would have planned our wedding. Father McLaughlin cautioned us to wait. He told us that this was all too quick and that our love would only blossom with time."

That night Robert penned a letter to his girlfriend at home. Dolly and he had dated a few times in high school and Dolly had been his date for the graduation dance. After acknowledging to himself that he missed her, Robert asked, "Do you think we might get married some day? When we met at Christmas I wanted to ask you but I thought it might scare you off. But now that we are preparing to leave for the war front, it would be a comfort to know you'd be waiting for me to return home to start a life together." Robert had always been impetuous and straightforward. A few days before leaving Fort Pickett by Route 40 to catch a troop ship out of Norfolk, Dolly answered in the affirmative and promised to wait for him.

Round Corners

Book Seven

Round Corners

Book Seven

Chapter Thirty-seven

Unearthing new evidence:

The day after the storm the city of New Bedford was lit by a bright sun. Its citizens were grateful that they had escaped the ravages of the wind and surf. Detective Bill Normandin informed Inspector O'Malley: "the earth samples taken from the Spooner property did not contain a particular unique mineral found with the skeletal remains. When David Rubin informed Doctor Ralph Malcolm that the Spooner family had owned a summer residence in upstate New York at Saratoga Springs, the professor highly suggested that a sampling be taken of that property. The chemical elements associated with these springs are deposited into the top layers of the ground cover."

"So, Doctor Malcolm is suggesting that there would probably be a match to the mineral that was uncovered. Am I right?" asked O'Malley. "Yes," answered Bill. "And if such a match could be made, it would be extremely helpful and would be supporting evidence as to where these human remains were buried prior to being inserted in the walls of the New Bedford residence."

"Is David Rubin requesting a local coroner's office or police department to get and forward earth samples from that property," inquired O'Malley. "No," answered Bill. "He has decided to travel to upstate New York to retrieve the samples himself. He told me that in his first years in college he worked as a busboy and then waiter at some of the prestigious summer hotels in the Catskills. On his few days off during those summer months, he and other co-workers would travel to the Saratoga Racetrack. He's very familiar with the area and relishes going back to make a visit, the weekend after Columbus Day. He's invited me to come along."

"You and David have certainly hit it off," commented O'Malley.

Columbus Day, October 12th, fell on a Wednesday. David had informed Bill that he planned to drive to the Grossinger's Resort Hotel and to stay there overnight. "If we leave before noon on Friday, we should easily make the approximately two hundred miles and be there in time for dinner. When I contacted Mr. Asher Grossinger's daughter, Jennie, about my coming into the area, she invited us for dinner and free lodging. Her mother, known to their guests as Malke, operates one of the finest kosher kitchens in Sullivan County. The hotel only has a skeleton crew this time of year mostly doing repairs. There are occasional groups who come to the hotel for meetings but these Catskill hotels are filled to the brim in the summer months with guests who are escaping the heat of New York City."

On the drive that brought them through Worcester, Springfield and the Berkshire mountains in Massachusetts, David described the summers he spent in the Catskills. "There are many hotels and they mostly cater to Jewish families. They specialize in providing the best kosher foods. You haven't tasted anything better than a sample from a towering shoal of gefilte fish or the potato pudding. The days are spent relaxing around the large veranda porches or plying the lakes in a canoe or row boat. In the evening the entertainment is as good as any club in Manhattan. The Grossinger Hotel where I worked my first summer as a busboy had such celebrities as Eddie Canter and Irving Berlin. Milton Berle came each summer to the Concord for rest and relaxation but would entertain the guests one night while he was in residence. He was such a funny guy."

A little after four o'clock David Rubin and Bill Normandin were driving through the gates of the 100 acre property of the

Grossinger Resort. They proceeded to the Terrace Hill House which was the original building on the resort and the residence of the Grossinger family. A number of other buildings had been added over the years and a new athletic building was in the last stage of construction. Jennie came out to greet the two young men. "How good it is to see you, David," she exclaimed. "It's been over three years since my last visit," stated David. He introduced Bill, "This is Detective Bill Normandin. He's a colleague who is assisting on a case back in New Bedford, MA. I am presently working in the local coroner's office. New Bedford is located on the route to Cape Cod."

"Come in," Jennie invited. "My father is back in Manhattan on some business but my mother is anxiously waiting to see you." David and Bill picked up their small valises from the trunk of the Chrysler De Soto Coupe and followed Jennie into the house. "Just put those down for now. I'll show you to your rooms later," said Jennie. "We'll go see mother first. And as you might suspect," she continued as she look at David, "she's in the kitchen."

Mrs. Grossinger was working at a table in the center of the room and facing the entrance. As she looked up and saw David, she wiped her hands on a towel, removed her clean white apron and with the biggest smile came over to greet him with a big hug. "It's so good to see you, David. It's been too long."

After greeting Bill, Mrs. Grossinger explained: "the menu for our meal tonight includes, Cider-Dijon pork chops with roasted sweet potatoes and apples. The dessert is a surprise and one of David's favorites." Inquisitive Bill Normandin not familiar with Jewish customs inquired "David told me that you have one of the finest kosher kitchens in the Catskills. What makes it kosher?"

"Oh, boy!" remarked all three almost in unison. Mrs. Grossinger looked smilingly at David and her Jennie, "You have brought an infidel into our midst. I see that he has a lot to learn about our religious traditions. We will have to proceed slowly."

"The Torah list the animals that are considered ritually clean from those that are unclean," started David. "Also only the meat from an animal which has been slaughtered according to Jewish law can be used in a kosher kitchen," continued Mrs. Grossinger. "The preparation of a kosher meal requires knowledge of the ingredients but also a cleanliness that assures that nothing gets contaminated in the process," she continued. "What I can assure you, Bill," remarked Jennie, "is that my mother's food will be delicious as well as healthy."

After being shown to his room, Bill Normandin looked out over the lake from his window. A bright moon was playing on the wrinkles of the lake that had arisen with a refreshing breeze. He was grateful for David's friendship and his willingness to introduce him to a whole new culture and customs.

During the evening meal, the conversation included a reference to David's "Bar Mitzvah." Upon questioning from Bill, David explained, "A Jewish boy automatically becomes a bar mitzvah when he reaches 13 years of age. Under Jewish Law, children are technically not obligated to observe the commandments. The bar mitzvah, which can be associated with a religious service, publicly marks the assumption of these obligations. At the Shabbat service following my 13th birthday, I was called up by the Rabbi to the Torah and asked to recite a blessing over the weekly readings. I was now considered old enough to be held responsible for my own actions. On that day I was considered a man. My father recited a blessing grateful that the burden of being responsible for my sins had been lifted from his shoulders."

When Jennie and her mother went to the kitchen to get the dessert, Bill asked David, "What's your favorite dessert?" "I'm not sure," answered David. "All of Mrs. Grossinger's desserts are memorable.

I've been trying to figure out which one she is referring to ever since she mentioned it in the kitchen."

As Mrs. Grossinger placed the dessert on the table, David exclaimed, "It's a Shabbat torte. And from the aroma it contains peaches, my favorite fruit." Looking over to Bill, Jennie explained, "A Shabbat torte has many variations depending on the fruit used in its preparation. Some include plums, apricots and of course apples and blueberries or even a mixture of these fruit. Mother remembered that the peach torte was David's favorite. Enjoy!"

After dessert and coffee, David insisted that he and Bill would assist in clearing the table. Bill announced, "I'll help your mother to wash the dishes and clean the kitchen. Jennie, you and David have a lot of catching up. Plus, I have many questions for your mother." Bill had recognized a certain glow that emanated from David and Jennie when they looked at each other from across the table. It was even more evident as they moved close to each other as they brought items from the dining room to the kitchen.

David remarked, "Thank you, Bill. We need to be off early tomorrow." Looking at Jennie, David said, "Let's get our coats and go for walk down to the lake. It's getting a bit cold out but should be comfortable enough."

After plying Jennie's mother with many questions, Bill announced that he would retreat to his room. "It's been a long day. And there are so many new thoughts and information in my head that I need some time to put some order to them."

It was much later that evening that Bill, almost asleep in his bed, heard David in the room that was adjacent. Bill smiled as he lay there. He was happy for David.

Round Corners

Chapter Thirty-eight

Around nine o'clock the next morning, Jennie and her mother were saying goodbye to their guests. Mrs. Grossinger had provided a hearty breakfast. Bill recognized the scrambled eggs and fruit salad. Mrs. Grossinger pointed out to Bill, "These are cheese blintzes and are filled with cottage cheese. It's an old recipe from Poland." As she recalled her ancestry, her eyes filled with tears. "It's so terrible what we are hearing from our people back home. It sounds like Hitler and the Nazis are out to destroy us. We are hearing that the work camps that our people are being forcibly brought to are in fact death camps. They are starved, beaten and worked to death and then cremated in huge ovens."

Jennie rose from her chair at the kitchen table where breakfast was being served and kissed her mother on the forehead trying to erase these terrible thoughts that plagued her. "Enough," said Mrs. Grossinger as she took hold of herself. "Let us enjoy our friends."

Turning again to Bill, she explained that there was a side dish that is very popular at breakfast time and pointed to a piece of smoked salmon. "A small piece of lox garnished with tomato, red onion and cucumber is a delicacy that is a great compliment to the cheese blintzes and eggs," she said and encouraged Bill to try some. When Bill tasted the lox he was surprised that he found the unusual introduction of fish into a breakfast menu was quite agreeable. "Very good," he exclaimed.

Jennie bent down to the open window of David's yellow coupe and kissed him farewell. "Don't be such a stranger, David. Come back soon."

Silence accompanied the travelers as they left the Grossinger resort and headed upstate to Saratoga. The distance was less than 80 miles but it would take them about three hours, as they had to drive through the state capital of Albany. Eventually, Bill broke into the silence. "You're very sweet on Jennie, aren't you?" asked Bill.

"You noticed," smiled David. "We had known each other when I worked at the Grossinger a few years back. We were friends but I kept a safe distance. After all, she was my employer's daughter. I didn't realize until last night that we had deep feelings for each other back then and it seemed to blossom as we were together last night."

Once the ice was broken, David couldn't stop talking, recollecting his summers at the resorts in the Catskills. "It was such a happy and carefree time," stated David. "We worked hard and always had to present ourselves well with the guest. Most were friendly and out to enjoy some time in the country, but of course, there were always those who were hard to please. The sun was too hot. The umbrella didn't provide enough shade. The food was cold. A neighbor was too loud. You get the idea?" asked David.

"Each summer," continued David, "we drove up to the Saratoga Racetrack at least once. One summer we were able to squeeze in two visits. Three out of the four of us had come back winners and we were just itching to return. We managed another visit before the track closed for the season. As you can imagine we left a substantial donation at the track and came away with only a minute amount of our tips that we had so carefully saved for the occasion. It was a learning experience."

"On a nice summer day, there is no better venue than attending a horse race," commented David. "At Saratoga hardly anyone are in the stands. There is a large viewing area where one sees these beautiful animals, the trainers and colorfully dressed jockeys. I still feel the excitement when I remember hearing: "Riders Up.""

"However, we are going to Saratoga for a totally different reason," exclaimed David. "I researched the address of the former summer home of Mrs. Spooner. It's not far from the Saratoga Spa that was built by Franklin Delano Roosevelt. Do you know where that is?" inquired Bill. "I'm familiar with a resort close by to the Spa. It had a lush golf course," answered David.

"I've read," continued David, "that Victoria Pool built at the Saratoga Spa State Park has an outdoor heated pool. Probably it's the first one in the country. When President Roosevelt was governor of New York he became a strong proponent of the healthful environments of the springs in Saratoga. There are over a dozen mineral springs in Saratoga County. They are naturally carbonated and no two springs taste exactly alike. Each one produces its own unique mineral contents, imparting its own distinctive flavor. From my research I believe the closest spring to the Spooner residence is either Polaris Spring or Hathorn Spring."

Around noontime David drove into the heart of Saratoga Springs. He pointed out, "that's Congress Park. Columbian Spring, I believe, is the most popular spring in the park but there is at least one other one. We drove by here on our way to the race track which is only a few miles away. However, if I remember correctly the Saratoga Spa is to the west and somewhat further. Let's find the Spooner summer home first and if we have time I'll show you the racetrack. We have lots of work to do and it's a long ride home from here."

With the assistance of the local post mistress, David received direction to the Spa and a property that she remembered had belonged to a family from the Cape Cod area of Massachusetts. When they reached their destination, David and Bill discovered that the summer residence was already closed for the winter months. "We just can't go on the property," stated Bill who was now assuming his role as a police detective. "Let's see if there are any neighbors still in town."

An elderly gentleman drove into a driveway just next door. Bill approached him and briefly explained the nature of his visit and the interest they had in the neighboring property. Mr. Richard Talbot introduced himself, "I never met the previous owner, but I had learned that she was a woman from Massachusetts. Her chauffeur, Mr. Bloom, and I would meet in the neighborhood and occasionally at the race track."

Bill inquired about the present owners and learned that it belonged to an elderly couple. "The Weissenbergs, Alexis and his wife, Hilda, have a primary residence on Long Island and spend most of the winter in southern Florida," related Mr. Talbot. "Is there anyone in town who could give us permission to take a few samples from the grounds of that property?" inquired Bill. "My companion is a scientist who is conducting a study of earth samples and the mineral composition that it contains. He is focusing on the effects of the mineral springs found in this County of New York."

"Let me give the Weissenbergs a call," volunteered Mr. Talbot. "My wife, Jeanne, was on the phone with Hilda just before I left for the market. They're still on Long Island and preparing to travel to Florida right after the Thanksgiving weekend."

Mr. Talbot removed a bag of groceries from his shiny Chrysler Crown Imperial. He pointed out some features of his recent purchase, "this Chrysler model has fluid drive, over drive and power brakes. This year sealed-beamed headlights became standard equipment." "It's a beauty," exclaimed David Rubin, as he moved his hand over the smooth finish. "Just wait here. I'll be right out," stated Mr. Talbot.

A few minutes later, Mr. Talbot returned. Bill noticed that he had a slight limp to his walk and inquired, "Are you suffering from an old injury?" "Most of this halting walk is due to old age," answered Mr. Talbot with a smile. "In our younger days my wife and I used to do a lot of mountain climbing. We are proud to tell people that we walked a major portion of the northern section of the Appalachian Trail. But now the knees just won't cooperate."

"Alexis is a retired science professor in the New York school system," stated Mr. Talbot. "He is more than agreeable that you access his property to conduct your research. He would be grateful if you would share the results of your study. He asked me to accompany you, so that I may give him a report of your activity. Would that present a problem?" inquired Mr. Talbot.

"Absolutely not," answered David. Together they walked back to the property once occupied by Mrs. Spooner. David removed a few tools from the trunk of his automobile. David inquired from Mr. Talbot, "What Spring is closest to this property? Is it Polaris or Hathorn? The maps are less than conclusive." "As a crow flies, the Polaris is certainly the closest. There's a marsh that separates our properties from that Spring. It takes less than fifteen minutes to walk to the Hathorn Spring since it's a direct route to the west of here. A walk around the marsh to the Polaris would take about a half hour and with these knees, maybe closer to an hour."

David handed the tools to Bill to carry as he took out a notebook and entered the information that Mr. Talbot had shared with them. "Most of the properties on this side of the street that abuts the marsh are about an acre in size," informed Mr. Talbot. The front of the property consisted of a small well maintained lawn and a driveway similar to the one on Mr. Talbot's property. Most of the property was to the rear of the comfortable summer residence. Mr. Talbot pointed out the slated covered patio under an umbrella of trees, "That is where the Weissenbergs entertained most of their guest during the warm summer days. We were privileged to be frequent visitors and met so many of their friends who travelled up from New York," contributed Mr. Talbot. "My wife, Jeanne, is a writer for various magazines. She picked up many intriguing ideas from these engaging conversations. She would have more than enough material to keep her busy all winter long. It inspired one of her best known pieces that appeared in the New Yorker magazine. It was entitled "Summer Conversations."

David drifted away from the group and walked along the perimeter of the property all the while observing the contour of the land. He made some entries into his notebook. He called out, "Bill, bring the tools to this area. I want to take a sample of this section." Bill, who had previously joined David, taking samples at the former Spooner residence knew the routine. First, with a small spade he removed the grass covering about a foot in circumference and laid it aside. David pointed out to Mr. Talbot that, "we will replace this grass once we have abstracted our earth sample. This instrument is used to bore into the ground. You'll notice that the center is empty. Once we reach a depth of at least a foot, we will retract the instrument and collect the earth sample. If the earth is damp and holds together, we carefully place it in our container indicating the portion that is closest to the surface. Sometime the minerals from the Springs are airborne and at other times they are moving through the earth. Often it is both. It would interest me to learn whether the particular component mineral of the Polaris Spring has travelled through the marsh."

After declining an invitation to share some liquid refreshments with Mr. Talbot and his wife, David Rubin and Bill Normandin headed to the Saratoga racetrack. When Mr. Talbot had mentioned that he had met Mr. Bloom, the chauffeur, at the racetrack when Mrs. Spooner was in residence both had glanced at each other and had arrived at similar conclusions. David stated excitedly, "The Big Red Spring burbles, from the ground, near the paddock at the back of the picnic area."

Around three o'clock David and Bill started their return trip to New Bedford. After going through Albany and entering into Massachusetts, both decided they needed to have something to eat. The fine breakfast prepared by Mrs. Grossinger was well digested by then. They came across a Howard Johnson restaurant near Greenfield. Sitting at the counter, David ordered a burger and fries plate while Bill ordered a cup of New England clam chowder and a BLT on bread toasted on the grill. "We have to keep room for the ice cream," exclaimed Bill. "I'm told that the ice cream is far richer than anything else on the market. It has twice the butterfat and uses all-natural flavorings." "I've read," added David, "that Mr. Johnson bought the recipe from an elderly German pushcart vendor."

Round Corners

Chapter Thirty-nine

While Bill Normandin was in upstate New York, Inspector Daniel O'Malley had made arrangements to meet Mr. Horace Bloom at the Portnoy home in the west end of the city. He parked his unmarked vehicle about a block away. As he exited the vehicle he turned up the collar of his light weight trench coat and pulled down on his fedora. The rains and wind blowing off the bay were heavy.

Mr. Bloom greeted the Inspector at the front door. After placing the hat and coat on a stand in the hallway, Mr. Bloom invited O'Malley to follow him. "I want to introduce you to my employers, Mr. & Mrs. Portnoy," he announced. The elderly couple was reading the morning paper in an adjacent room.

"Mr. and Mrs. Portnoy, as I mentioned to you earlier, this is Inspector O'Malley from the downtown police headquarters. He wishes to ask me a few questions about my previous employment with Mrs. Spooner." Mr. Portnoy had risen from his chair and introduced himself, "Please call me George and this is Evelyn," as he pointed to his wife. George Portnoy was a tall, thin man and though giving the appearance of being weak and sickly, grasped O'Malley's hand with a firm grip.

Horace Bloom excused himself and asked the Inspector to follow him. They went to an adjacent room. It was the clearly the dining room. Two dining room chairs had been set in the corner of the room and provided some privacy for their conversation.

O'Malley invited Mr. Bloom to take a seat. He had noticed that Horace Bloom was reluctant to be informal with him and only seated himself after the Inspector had taken his seat. "I understand from

Mrs. Spooner that you were in her employ for many years. Is that correct?" asked the Inspector.

Horace Bloom was a big man, about the same six foot height of O'Malley but with a much broader frame. O'Malley had judged that Horace was at least sixty years of age yet his wide, strong shoulders portrayed him as much younger. "Yes," answered Mr. Bloom. "Prior to coming to New Bedford, I had worked for Mr. David Weigand's family in New York. Soon after Mr. Weigand's marriage to Lady Spooner, he had offered me employment at their home in New Bedford. Along with being chauffeur, my duties included that of gardener, handy man around the house and watchman of those in the household. As the director of the garment factory on the west side of New York City that produced very popular women's dresses, he was away from his New Bedford home for long stretches of time. David's father still owned the business but for all practical matters David ran the business."

"According to Mrs. Spooner, she and David had one son, Mortimer. She told me that he was quite sickly as a young boy and had a troubled relationship with his father. Is that how you would describe it?" asked the Inspector.

"Even as a child, Mortimer seemed a disappointment to his father," agreed Mr. Bloom. "I suspect that Mr. Weigand had anticipated having a son that was strong in body and will, much like himself. Unfortunately, Mortimer was sickly as a child and Mrs. Spooner just fawned over him. This just drove Mr. Weigand to have many heated exchanges with his wife over her handling of his son. These outbursts could be heard throughout the house. Mortimer would scamper away and hide. Even at a very young age he grasped that he was at the center of his parent's disagreements."

"Mortimer became sullen and moody. He hardly smiled and kept to himself," continued Mr. Bloom. "Mrs. Spooner bought her

Mortimer a small dog, a mixed white poodle when he was about six years of age. Mortimer loved that dog and spent all his time with her. However, I began to suspect that Mortimer abused his dog especially when his father was home. Mortimer never received a word of praise from his father. Even when Mr. Weigand seemed to try to encourage his son, it came out as a criticism. That's when I would hear cries and yelps of pain coming from Mortimer's room. When I approached Mortimer on the subject, he only closed his eyes and ignored me."

"Around that time he began to carve his initial M on the back of his left hand," stated Mr. Bloom. "I brought this to Mrs. Spooner's attention and carefully suggested that her son needed some professional assistance. I had read that someone who cuts at his own skin is exhibiting signs of mental imbalance."

"Did Mrs. Spooner follow your advice?" asked O'Malley.

"At first, I believe she was in denial," answered Mr. Bloom. "But as she saw the scars of the initial M becoming more pronounced, I know she sought some medical help. On a few occasions I drove the two of them to appointments to a doctor known for his expertise in mental illness."

"There was one discovery that made me fearful for our safety," stated Horace Bloom with a look of horror on his face. "One of my duties around the house was to handle the coal-fired boiler in the winter. One evening while I was shoveling coal into the open boiler, I came across the remains of Mortimer's dog. His white fur was blackened and bones were evidently broken by the crush of coal that covered the dog. About a month earlier we had received a supply of coal. The truck backs up to the open window, a chute is placed from the back of the truck to the window and as the driver hydraulically lifts the rear of the truck, coals tumbles down into the cellar usually a ton at each delivery."

Horace Bloom began to breathe heavily and said shakily, "I had met with the driver and noticed that Mortimer and his dog were hanging around that side of the house. I then went into the cellar to make sure that the partition that kept the coal from flowing into the open cellar was in place. When I returned I remembered that Mortimer and the dog were gone. I thought nothing of it until I found the dog's crushed body in the coal. Mortimer's dog went missing the day of the coal delivery. When Mrs. Spooner, Mrs. Moriarity or I asked Mortimer about his dog, he didn't seem to care and what was becoming a more frequent habit, he would close his eyes and just walk away. From the height of the coal chute, there is no way Mortimer's dog could have accidently reached that chute." With beads of sweat on his forehead at this recollection, Horace Bloom stated, "Mortimer had to put his own dog on that chute."

"How terrible," expressed Inspector O'Malley. "As you concluded earlier, Mortimer showed signs of being a very sick young man."

Round Corners

Chapter Forty

O'Malley appreciated the difficulty that Mr. Bloom was having in revealing this knowledge he had about young Mortimer Spooner, or had he retained his father's name of Weigand? "Do you want to take a break?" asked the Inspector. "It has stopped raining. We could go for a walk around the neighborhood," suggested O'Malley.

"No, I'll be fine," answered Mr. Bloom. "However, let's go to the kitchen. There is always a pot of coffee on the stove. Would you like to join me in a cup?" asked Horace Bloom.

The kitchen was empty so Horace and Daniel O'Malley sat at the small kitchen table drinking some pretty strong coffee. "I understand from Mrs. Spooner that Mortimer went away to a boarding school in New Hampshire. Do you recall how Mortimer fared while he was away at school?" asked the Inspector.

"I don't know the details," answered Mr. Bloom, "but Mrs. Spooner indicated that Mortimer had a very difficult first year at the boarding school. However, for the following three years she received only glowing reports from the headmaster. Young Mortimer changed dramatically right before our eyes. He began to excel in his studies and became very proficient in tennis, track and cross country skiing. I would drive our lady to these athletic events along with other members of the household – that is Mrs. Moriarity and her daughter. Those were happy days for Mrs. Spooner who had finally divorced Mr. Weigand."

"Did Mr. Weigand keep in contact with his son either in New Bedford or at the New Hampshire school during the time after the divorce?" asked O'Malley.

"Not to my knowledge," answered Horace Bloom. "He didn't even come to Mortimer's graduation. The only time I saw them in each other's company was at the Saratoga racetrack in upstate New York. Mrs. Spooner had purchased a summer home in Saratoga Springs where the entire household would spend over ten weeks in the country every summer. I enjoyed going to the races and introduced Mrs. Moriarity's granddaughter, Maureen, to the sport. She just loved the horses and would spend hours around the stables helping the handlers. Because of her enthusiasm, Mortimer agreed to come with us. He also became enamored with these fine animals. It was at one of these visits to the track that Mr. Weigand and his son met purely by accident. They were cordial to each other but distant. I don't know whether they ever met again."

Round Corners

Chapter Forty-one

On Monday morning following the trip to upstate New York, Detective Bill Normandin met with Inspector Daniel O'Malley. The evening before he had left a message that he would be late for their usual nine o'clock get-together. David Rubin and he had not returned to New Bedford until three o'clock in the morning. Even though he was exhausted, he found he couldn't sleep. There were too many items of information running through his head and he couldn't wait to share them with his superior. So at eight he was up; he cleaned up from the grime of the previous day and headed out to meet the Inspector in the downtown police station.

Inspector O'Malley looked up surprised, "I wasn't expecting you until later this morning."

Bill told how he was not able to sleep and that he just wanted to share his findings and hear what the Inspector had learned from Mrs. Spooner's former chauffeur as well as any other development that may have come up in the case.

Bill told O'Malley, "David is driving up the earth samples to the Boston lab later today. He's assumed that the small samples of earth discovered with the skeletal remains have already been analyzed. Plus the samples from the Spooner residence on County Street should also have been compared by now. He is staying over with his family in Newton and plans to analyze the samples taken in Saratoga tomorrow. We took samples at the Spooner summer home as well as at the racetrack. We discovered that Mr. Bloom spent considerable time at the track each summer."

Inspector O'Malley related his findings, "My inquiries with Mr. Bloom were very enlightening and quite disturbing. Mortimer was very unsound in his youth. He inflicted cuts on his body and Mr. Bloom suspects that Mortimer was responsible for the death his own dog. As Mortimer grew up, these disturbing signs and incidences ended. Presently, he is doing very well at the Naval Academy in Annapolis, Maryland. I've requested copies of his fingerprints from the military files and should receive them by Wednesday. We will match them against those found on and in the box that contained the skeletal remains."

Detective Normandin continued, "By Friday we may have some answers to our mystery."

Round Corners

Book Eight

Round Corners

Book Eight

Chapter Forty-two

Into the battle:

After basic training and a brief stay with his family, Claude was again saying farewell to Anne, his girlfriend. This time the mood was extremely somber. He had been assigned to the Naval Base at Port Hueneme in California. There he was to continue his training awaiting an expected assignment of his battalion to an island in the Pacific.

Claude and Tom Singleton met again at the railway station in Providence. On the way to the West Coast additional members of the Seabees battalion that had recently completed their basic training gradually filled the three railroad cars that had been assigned for their use. Almost all came on board wearing the Dress White uniform, equipped with a dark blue neckerchief that they had received at the completion of basic training. They were extremely sharp looking. In New York Ralph "Grubby" Papaleo got on the train wearing his Dress Blue uniform. Claude explained to Tom, "Here's a mate who doesn't trust himself to keep his white uniform clean."

For the remainder of the trip the three men were inseparable. Again Grubby provided all types of food for the road. Along with his Seabag, Grubby carried a huge sack on board. He had come prepared for a long journey. The train travelled day and night making occasional stops to pick up passengers and fuel. Boxed meals were provided three times a day but the real treats were in Grubby's sack. He shared willingly with anyone nearby.

Grubby had also brought a few decks of playing cards. Before long most of the men in Grubby's railroad car were seated on the floor in the aisles and playing poker or pitch. Money was scarce so wagering consisted mostly of cigarettes.

In Chicago the three railroad cars with Seabees were dropped off at a siding while another locomotive was attached for the final push to the California coast. Port Hueneme was a deep water port between the Port of Los Angeles and the Port of San Francisco.

In Omaha, Nebraska John Winters came aboard. Tom Singleton had been together with John during the rifle training sessions at Camp Peary. Tom informed his mates, "John is a marksman. He would regularly hit the center of the target, 5 out of 5 times, with hardly any effort."

John Winters explained, "My experience in shooting started early in the days I lived in the hills of Tennessee. At age seven my granddaddy gave me a single shot rifle that was as big as I was then. We would go squirrel and coon hunting. I quickly learned to take down a raccoon. They move rather slowly and can be a good sized target. The squirrels were a challenge but before long I could drop one as he ran away or up a tree."

"When I was a teenager," continued John, "the family moved to western Nebraska. My father purchased a plot of land and decided that farming would provide the family a good financial future. However, when the dust started to blow a few years ago, we lost everything. Our family stayed on the land. Most of our neighbors packed all their belongings on rickety old Model T vehicles and trekked out to the west hoping to find work. We heard later that many never made it. Many died along the way. We were lucky. My Dad had found work in Omaha. He would be away for weeks at a time. My mother and we older kids fought the sand filled clouds that would come blowing through. Fortunately, my granddaddy had dug us a deep well and hit a vein that kept the family going through the driest days."

After five days of train travel, the Seabees arrived at their destination. They hadn't bathed during the journey, so it was a pretty ripe group who entered the gates of the naval base at the port of Hueneme. For the first time they appreciated the Seabag and its contents that they had received upon the successful completion of basic training. It contained clean underwear, towels, socks, trousers and jumpers, shoes and even a pillow slip and a whisk broom. A dark blue pea coat right now just added weight but was available for colder weather.

The next day, assignments were given to the men. Claude Lepage was assigned to kitchen duty. In the next few weeks he peeled endless bags of potatoes. After washing pots and pans, he finished each day washing down the kitchen and mess hall floors. The men he worked with were good sports. They sang as they peeled potatoes, and Joe Foster had more stories and jokes to relate that were far-fetched but entertaining.

One day back in the barracks, Grubby told his bunk mates, "I overheard one of the commanding officers waiting for his jeep talking about upcoming assignments off the coast of Australia. There's a troop ship in New York that's ready to sail to India, via the South Atlantic route. From there it is shipping out to New Zealand. It sounds like they expect the ship to arrive on the West Coast in about three months. We will be a construction support group for the Marines who are occupying some islands off the coast of Australia."

Tom Singleton who had been assigned to office duty filled in some further details, "The ship was originally a cruise ship, but it was called into service by the Navy. The ship has been named the USS West Point. At the Norfolk Ship Yards it was converted into a troop ship. Life-rafts cover the promenade deck windows, "standee bunks" can be found everywhere, anti-aircraft guns have been installed, and it was painted a camouflage gray color. I was told that the ships troop-carrying capacity is over seven thousand."

Claude Lepage informed the men that he was being trained to be a cook, "It looks like I have a few months to become a chef. Some of the islands we are being sent to belong to the French. Most of the native population speaks French. I was told that my ability to speak French could be helpful in making contact with the local people in order to get fresh produce, milk and other items. These islands seemingly don't have stores like we have at home."

Early the next morning as Claude was heading off to the kitchen, Grubby called out, "Have a good day, Frenchie. If you need any help in making a menu, I'm your man." By nightfall all his mates in the barracks had picked up on Claude's new nickname and it would last throughout his years in the service.

Round Corners

Chapter Forty-three

The USS West Point pulled into the port of Hueneme. There was a certain excitement among the Seabees who made up the Naval Construction Battalion. The battalion was composed of 750 men, divided into three companies of 250 men each.

Petty Officers Tom Singleton and John Winters belonged to Company B. Frenchie and Grubby were temporarily assigned to Company A. Because of their expertise, they were told that their assignment would be decided once they arrived closer to the islands off the coast of Australia.

The Seabees were given a rare shore leave the evening prior to shipping out. The company of four headed out to a bar that overlooked one of the shipping piers next to the naval base. Grubby, the city boy, and John Winters, the farm boy, loved looking out over the waves crashing onto the shore just south of the pier. Frenchie and Tom Singleton were accustomed to the ocean that bordered their home towns on the East Coast.

Grubby's mates had tried to convince him to wear his Whites and had him almost convinced. Tim Singleton had even stated, "From what I hear we won't have an occasion to wear our dress Whites on the islands." Just before leaving on Liberty, Grubby changed into his dress Blues and promised, "When we come back to this coast after our tour of duty, I promise to wear my dress Whites on our first shore leave." As he said those words, all wondered silently whether they would all return safely from the war zone.

Two girls dressed in slacks that Katherine Hepburn had modeled to publicize the Broadway version of "The Philadelphia Story" approached the foursome. The three dashing young men in Dress Whites had caught their attention but it was Grubby's wide smile and the comfortable way he spoke with them that had the two girls circling around him.

In a period of only five days the ship was loaded with troops, mostly Marines. There were a few pieces of heavy equipment on the deck but most of the construction material that was to be used in the construction of bases for the Marines had already been shipped out on cargo ships. Filled with provisions for a two week voyage, the USS West Point left the harbor under escort.

The Navy Seabees were assigned an area at the aft of the ship. John Winters commented, "We are very dependent upon our escort. Basically we are a large floating target for the Japanese fighter planes and U boats." He crossed himself and the men around did the same, even those who were not particularly religious.

Claude Lepage, having a rare hangover, found the movement of the ship as it got underway did not agree with him. But the extra drinks he had with his mates before leaving the bar was not the only cause. He didn't have sea legs and was seasick for the whole ten day trip. Grubby was fine and took advantage of the situation, eating most of Frenchie's unfinished portions of grub.

The men aboard ship observed some battle activities at a distance on the horizon but the USS West Point and its escort continued safely toward its destination.

A day out from shore Claude learned that he would be landing as part of Company C on the island of New Caledonia. Two battalions of Marines were going offshore on the island. The Seabees in Company C were mostly trained in the construction of Quonset Huts. New barracks, an additional mess hall and officers' quarters were needed to be built to accommodate the influx of Marines. Tom Singleton and

John Winters were to be dropped off on the New Hebrides Islands. Both Company A and B were being assigned to expand the pontoon pier at Port Vila on New Hebrides. It was being developed to be an important staging point in battles to reclaim the many islands that the Japanese had quickly overrun. Grubby finally learned of his assignment when the heavy equipment aboard the USS West Point was unloaded on New Caledonia. Two days before their arrival, Grubby had been assigned to getting the engines tuned up and running. Frenchie was happy to have at least one of his buddies on the island.

Frenchie was sent to help the kitchen crew at Noumea. With the influx of additional Marines, an extra cook was very welcome. The Australians had helped secure the territory and it had quickly become an important Allied base. Noumea, the capital of New Caledonia, was designated the United States Navy and Army headquarters in the South Pacific.

The base was equipped with electricity from the huge generators that had been shipped from the U.S. Occasionally, one of the generators would go down and the cooks had to improvise the next meal. Frenchie greeted the men in the bakery, "I'm called Frenchie and I did have time to learn how to bake bread and rolls before shipping out." For ten hours a day, Frenchie and the bakery crew worked the dough, shaped countless loaves and rolls and received praise from the service men that could smell the aroma of fresh bread as they approached the mess hall.

The following Sunday Frenchie learned the particular difficulties that faced cooks on a distant island of the South Pacific. During an air raid warning, the kitchen generator went down. Someone had plugged the air raid system into the generator that also supported the kitchen. A large batch of bread had just been placed into the ovens. After an hour, the head chef barked out an order, "Pull out all the trays from the ovens and throw the half baked bread into clean barrels. Our men won't eat it but I know the local Kanakas will gratefully receive it to feed themselves or at least their pigs."

One night Grubby came into the barracks unusually late. When Frenchie first saw him, he didn't recognize who was coming toward him. All Frenchie could see were Grubby's eyes. "What happened to you?" asked Frenchie. Grubby answered with a grin, "We had one engine on a roller that just kept on backfiring. I had to strip down the whole engine to get it spinning like a top, but not before it backfired on me any number of times."

Round Corners

Chapter Forty-four

Mortimer's final year at the Academy went by very quickly. Even though the United States under Franklin Delano Roosevelt had remained out of the war in Europe and the Pacific, a heightened sense of preparation for military action was present in all the service academies. Richard attempted to find time to play his daily match of tennis with Mort, but his duties as Brigade Commander made it increasingly difficult to schedule a time when both would be available.

In May of 1941 Mortimer graduated and received a Bachelor of Science degree in the area of Engineering and Weapons, known as Division 1. None of his family attended the graduation ceremony. He accepted the fact that his mother was not well and travelling to Annapolis would have been too strenuous. His father had excused himself telling Mortimer that he would be travelling to the West Coast. He did send him a formal note of congratulations.

There were two rays of unexpected sunshine in what could have been a hollow accomplishment. Maureen, Mrs. Moriarity's daughter, who had married and lived in Maryland, had sent him a photograph of her family. Maureen had married Bob Farley, the assistant trainer, of the prestigious Foxcatcher Farm in Maryland owned by William DuPont, Jr. Maureen had met Bob while working at the thoroughbred race track in Saratoga. In the picture Maureen was holding a little, chubby faced boy.

Mortimer reminisced about the happy summers he had spent with Maureen at the racetrack. They had walked the now famous Seabiscuit around the track after workouts. That summer, automobile entrepreneur Charles S. Howard, bought the horse for $8,000. Meanwhile DuPont's racing operation was managed by trainer Richard Handlen. He and his assistant, Bob Farley, carefully groomed their thoroughbred, Rosemont, who had the distinction of beating Seabiscuit in the 1937 Santa Anita Handicap, a match race. The Santa Anita Handicap was known as the "hundred grander". It was California's most prestigious race and worth over $125,000 to the winner.

Mortimer still vividly recalled the calling of the race when Seabiscuit met War Admiral in what sports' writer dubbed the "Match of the Century." The event was run at the Pimlico Race Course in Baltimore, Maryland. Trains were run from all over the country to bring fans to the race. The track was jammed solid with fans, from the grandstands to the infield. It was estimated that 40 million fans listened to the race on the radio.

Head-to-head races favor fast starters, and War Admiral's speed from the gate was well known. Seabiscuit had been skilled at holding with the pack before pulling ahead with a late burst of speed. Tom Smith secretly trained Seabiscuit to run against this hype. When the bell rang, Seabiscuit ran away from the Triple Crown champion. At the first turn he was leading by more than a length. Halfway down the backstretch, War Admiral started to cut into the lead, gradually pulling level with Seabiscuit, then slightly ahead. George Woolf, the jockey, following the advice of the trainer eased up on Seabiscuit, allowing the horse to see his rival, and then asked for more speed. Two hundred yards from the wire, Seabiscuit did what came naturally to him. He pulled away again and continued to extend his lead over the closing stretch. Despite War Admiral's running his best time for the distance, Seabiscuit won by four lengths.

Mortimer was happy for Maureen. She looked extremely happy. He had met her husband, Bob Farley, once. He was probably five years older than Maureen. He was pleased that she remembered him and that she had sent her congratulations to him. He hadn't seen her in more than four years.

The other ray of light was the smiling blue eyes of Darlene. She had come to the graduation ceremony with the Cuthberts. They had not corresponded in the year since their meeting in New York. He was ecstatic to know that someone was present for his graduation.

Lieutenant JG Mortimer Weigand received orders to report to the USS Little. It was a converted Wickes-class destroyer used to support US Navy amphibious operations. It had been reclassified as an APD, AP for transport and D for destroyer. He met up with the ship in Norfolk. Most of the conversion of the ship, which included removing two forward boilers with their smokestack, had been completed a year earlier. Accommodations for 200 troops were installed in the former engine spaces.

As the flagship for TransDiv 12 she departed for San Diego. Lieutenant JG Mortimer Weigand supervised the amphibious landing exercises. After the completion of this amphibious training, the USS Little steamed for the South Pacific. After a brief stay at Midway Island, the ship departed for New Caledonia to join the Solomons campaign. Supplies for American troops on Guadalcanal had been badly disrupted. High-speed destroyer-transports were called upon to remedy this shortage.

Round Corners

Chapter Forty-five

The news that the Seabees on New Caledonia received about the progress of the war in the Pacific Theater was minimal and dismal. Some days the number of meals to be served was suddenly decreased. That's how Frenchie would learn that a platoon of Marines had departed the base under the cover of darkness. One day the Seabees got word of the massacre of Australian military nurses on the island of Balka and they were ordered to carry their weapon to their worksites.

One day Grubby excitedly related to the men in the barracks, "A Marine Sargent was encouraging his platoon by telling them that B-25's had taken off from the USS Hornet and had raided Nagoya, Tokyo and Yokohama, Japan. Jimmy Doolittle led the bombing raid. We are finally bringing the fight to them." Except for an occasional air raid, life for Frenchie and Grubby fell into a daily routine.

One day the Navy officer in charge of food stores received the o.k. from Claude Lepage's commanding officer to have Frenchie assigned to him for a special mission. Commander Jeffrey informed Claude, "Our local source for fresh produce is being over taxed. I've been informed that the area around Bourail which is northwest of here has large savannahs and plains and weather that are very suitable for farming. I want you to join us in an expedition to the area. It is about a five hour ride from here. We will be travelling over rough terrain and will be leaving tomorrow at dawn. We will have two jeeps at our disposal with five Marines, Tom a local Kanaka who knows the area and languages of that part of the island, as well as you and me. Tom speaks French, understandable English and many of the local dialects. Frenchie, I need someone who will be able to assure me that

I have an accurate gist of the conversations Tom will be having with the locals on my behalf."

Claude was more than happy to experience some change in his routine. "I'll be happy to join you," stated Claude. "May I suggest that I ride along with Tom so that I can get familiar with some of nuances and patois that I have heard with other locals doing kitchen duty?"

Commander Jeffrey appreciated Claude's suggestion and stated, "I believe I've chosen the right man for this job."

After leaving the outskirts of Noumea, the roads at times were hardly passable. At intervals it consisted of dry heavy ruts followed by marshy road beds. They drove on the west side of the Grand Terre's central mountain range that divided the island. Two Marines drove the Jeeps and the other three Marines were dressed and equipped for combat. Everyone had their weapons with them except for Tom, the civilian. Over the five hour ride to Bourail, Claude became quite comfortable with understanding Tom. Along with gaining familiarity with Tom's French accent, his use of words and phrases, Claude quizzed him about the local names of vegetables. When they arrived at their destination, Claude felt assured in his role as translator and interpreter.

Tom introduced Commander Jeffrey to a council of four men who represented one of the larger farming villages of Bourail. Prior to entering any business discussions, two native women served a local drink to the group. Claude looked over to Tom who nodded. Claude whispered to the Commander, "It's alright. You may just want to go easy."

After much nodding and pleasantries, Commander Jeffrey made his pitch, "Our Naval Base, that is protecting your islands from foreign occupation by the Japanese, needs a new supply of vegetables for our servicemen." He paused, allowing Tom to address the leaders of the village. Claude listened attentively as Tom translated the Commander's message first in French and hopefully the same message in the native dialect.

Claude nodded to the Commander who continued, "We are ready to provide you a reasonable price or exchange for the bounty of your fields. We are not looking to deprive you of the local needs of your people."

The Commander welcomed the pleasant expressions on the faces of his hosts. After a period of interchange, the Commander quickly learned that his hosts would only settle for American currency and not the French francs. Also they wanted in exchange, engineering assistance in structuring their water supply that flowed from the Diahot River.

When Claude returned to the base he couldn't wait to see his friend, Grubby. After hours of being called Petty Officer Claude Lepage by Commander Jeffrey, Claude unwittingly addressed his friend, "Ralph, our mission was a success. A new supply of fresh vegetables will be available to feed our men."

Allied coastwatchers were stationed throughout the many islands in the Coral Sea that lay east of Australia and north of New Zealand. Their task was to report on any enemy movements or other suspicious activities that they observed in the vicinity of their stations. New Caledonia had many coastwatchers stationed at the extreme northern end of the island. Grubby became friendly with a few of these men who came to the naval base from their outposts for recuperation from diseases and treatment for infections.

Dakota, an American, told him, "We are all commissioned as Royal Australian Naval Volunteer Reserve officers. It's the belief that it might prevent us from being executed for espionage, if we are captured by the Japanese. My sources don't seem to substantiate this tactic. Japanese forces hardly ever take our level of military personnel as prisoners. Our men when captured are routinely executed and left at their outpost most likely as a message to the rest of us."

Grubby related to Claude, "The spotters on Guadalcanal Island plus our reconnaissance aircraft have seen significant increase in Japanese naval maneuvers around New Guinea and the Solomon Islands. My sources tell me that since we are situated at the southeastern edge of the Coral Sea, we may be next in line to see action. If the Japanese were to control the Coral Sea from its northern edge at Port Moresby in New Guinea to our port in Noumea, they would effectively cut the supply line between Australia and the U.S. It looks like it would reduce or eliminate Australia as a threat to Japanese positions in the South Pacific."

Round Corners

Chapter Forty-six

As the rumors of invasion quickly spread through the island of New Caledonia, the natives began to adorn the roofs of their houses with totems and masks in the hope of averting this danger. A large portion of the native population had been converted to Roman Catholicism by the French missionaries but ancient customs sprung back to life in such times.

The Navy chaplains assigned to New Caledonia were also extremely busy during this time of uncertainty. One Saturday Claude invited Grubby, "Let's go to the Catholic Mass tomorrow morning after breakfast has been served." Grubby agreed. They had both been to confession earlier that afternoon. Grubby stated, "Father Pete Dagnoli made going to confession easy. He didn't make any fuss about my not going to church for many years."

A large Allied naval fleet was being observed gathering along the coast of Noumea. American troops counted up to 50,000 men attached to the base. It exceeded the number of native and resident population. When the fog over the bay rose one morning, the fleet was nowhere to be seen.

A week later the news began to filter back to the island that the Japanese navy had been turned back at what was called the Battle of the Coral Sea. The natives as well as the military stationed on the base were relieved.

Having failed in their plan to extend their control to the south of the Coral Sea, the Japanese turned their efforts to Guadalcanal situated at its northern edge. They landed troops and began the construction of an airfield. A month later 6,000 U. S. Marines, many who had been temporarily housed at Noumea, landed on Guadalcanal and seized the airfield, surprising the island's 2000 Japanese defenders.

Both sides began landing reinforcements by sea. US destroyer-transports discharged stores and Marine Raiders on the Guadalcanal beaches that summer and continued to support the Marines. On an unusually dark night, the support patrol boats were observed by a Japanese surface destroyer force that turned their guns on the ADPs. Like the other US ships, the USS Little, opened fire on the enemy destroyers. Though outgunned, Lieutenant Mortimer Weigand encouraged his men who were manning nine AA guns fitted to the deck. In the conversion of the destroyers, the torpedo mounts had been removed to make room for landing crafts. Addressing no one in particular, Mortimer stated, "We sure could use those torpedo tubes now."

Two ADPs, the USS Little and the USS Gregory, took direct hits from salvos which left them helpless and on fire. The Japanese, to assure their kill, steamed between the two stricken ships firing shells and strafing survivors. Lieutenant Mortimer suffered shrapnel wounds and burns and was stranded in the water for eleven hours before being rescued.

Even with these victories, the Japanese forces were unable to overwhelm the Americans' defensive perimeter and retake the airfield. A few months later the Japanese who had become badly outnumbered were forced to evacuate its remaining troops except for those who remained hidden in the island's jungles.

Grubby, who always managed to have a source for the latest rumors, told Claude, "Word is that the U.S. is now planning extensive bombing raids here in the Pacific similar to the ones the Royal Air Force is raining down on Berlin. An extensive naval air force is now in the area and airstrikes will allow our forces to retake many of the islands now occupied by Japan. Eventually, we will see our forces bombing Tokyo."

However, the anticipated momentum through the islands of the South Pacific to the coast of mainland Japan was thwarted as the Americans experienced more kamikaze attacks from Japanese aircrafts.

In April 1945 the news of the sudden death of President Roosevelt reached New Caledonia. The president had just been reelected to another term a few months earlier. Claude shared his concerns with Grubby, "I'm not sure about this Harry Truman who is now our president. Roosevelt was reluctant to get us into the war but started preparing for it long before Pearl Harbor. He mobilized our factories and Ford and other auto companies are now using the same assembly line technology to produce jeeps, tanks and military vehicles. Truman is a farmer from Missouri. Does he have enough savvy to lead us through this war effort?"

Grubby agreed, "My sources tell me that Germany is on the verge of surrendering to the Allied forces. We are just now starting to put Japan on its heels. Will Truman be as committed to fight this war in the Pacific as Roosevelt and his Generals?"

Early in August to everyone's surprise, the Enola Gay dropped an extraordinarily powerful bomb on Hiroshima. It was called an atomic bomb and it inflicted tremendous destruction on the city and a huge loss of civilian lives. Another bomb was dropped on Nagasaki a few days later. When the Japanese were still slow to surrender, Truman ordered a massive conventional air raid on Tokyo.

Grubby came running into the bakery where Claude was working, he called out, "Someone put on the radio. Emperor Hirohito has just issued a command ordering Japanese forces to cease fire."

"This could mean that the war is over," one cook shouted. All cheered. "We may be soon on our way home," added Grubby.

178

Round Corners

Chapter Forty-seven

Ensign Martha Lepage had little time to get adjusted to the surroundings and protocols at her new assignment at the Oakland Naval Hospital. Ships returning from the Pacific were constantly bringing in wounded Marines and Navy personnel. An increasingly steady flow of ships carrying these men entered the San Francisco Bay crossing under the Bay Bridge. The hospital had opened in 1942 on the site of a previous golf course and country club which had closed during the Depression. It was located in the Oak Knoll section of Oakland and was often referred to as the Oak Knoll Naval Hospital.

Nurse Lepage was housed in a three story wooden dwelling reserved for nurses that had been quickly constructed to accommodate the growing number of medical personnel assigned to the hospital. It was located in the hills of the hospital grounds and commanded a great view of the bay. In Oakland the Marines were in charge of the Navy nurses' training. The Marine officers took their role seriously. There was lots of marching. She soon learned the importance of these drills. Once a month on a Saturday morning, every available nurse not on duty in full dress marched to an area of the parade grounds where Naval and Marine officers awarded medals to the wounded men convalescing at the hospital. Due to the extent of their injuries, many marines and sailors received the Purple Heart.

Lieutenant Roberta Keller welcomed Martha to the ward, "Ensign Lepage, you have been assigned to my ward. You will soon learn that this ward is reserved for enlisted men who have sustained head and spinal cord injuries. The rooms directly across from this nursing station are known as quiet rooms and house the most seriously injured patients. There is normally only one man to a room but presently, due to the large number of our patients with frightful head injuries, most have two to a room."

"Please, follow me," continued the Director of Nurses for the ward. Two large doors opened into an open ward with three rows of beds, two rows located at the side walls and one down the center. "As you can see, we are filled beyond capacity with wounded servicemen. Last month we were forced to put in a row of beds down the middle of the ward. We now care for 40 patients in this ward."

Lieutenant Keller and Martha walked down the ward greeting patients. With a broad and warm smile, Nurse Keller inquired, "How do you feel this morning? This is our new nurse, Martha Lepage. You will soon be seeing lots of her." Eventually they reached the end of the ward. Beyond a nursing station, they entered another room. The room contained bunk beds. "This room houses the patients that are well on their way to recovery and will soon be discharged and sent home to their families," informed Nurse Keller.

Martha Lepage spent the next four months caring for the patients in the ward. She was amazed at the resilience and determination of these service men. Some of the men who had received injuries to their spinal cord had been left paralyzed from the waist down. Even though it seemed that they would never walk again and would be confined to move about in a wheel chair, many continued to exhibit a great sense of humor. They challenged each other to achieve even small feats. With the aid of hospital corpsmen and nurses they pushed through severe pain just to rise from a chair and stand. Most patients showed that they preferred the assistance of the nurses dressed in their white starched uniforms that included white stockings and long white sleeves. They would find ways of holding a nurse around the waist and showed their gratitude by a peck on the cheek.

One Saturday morning, the Director of Nurses selected Martha to wheel Marine Corporal, Francis Bennett, to the parade ground to receive his medal for valor in combat. Martha had assisted the Corporal on the cross bars. She had told him after an exceptionally challenging exercise, "Corporal Bennett, you must have been quite the warrior and leader. The progress I have seen you make in walking across the length of the cross bars was totally unexpected. You have given a call to your fellow patients to respond and follow your lead."

Red Cross volunteers, mostly women, visited the wards daily and put together special functions. A patient's birthday was remembered and celebrated. Holidays provided opportunities to bring in some entertainment. On one occasion, the USO brought Victor Borge who entertained on his piano on the parade grounds. Everyone who could possibly attend his performance was brought to the field, some even in beds. Those who were prevented from being present were moved to the window closest to the activity, so that they could hear Victor's music and constant flow of humorist comments. The audience broke out in laughter when he fell off the piano bench playing a song with energetic exuberance. The laughter got louder when he took out two ends of an automotive seat belt from under the seat lid and buckled himself onto the beach, "for safety."

Usually once a month, nurses would receive special permission to leave the base. Martha joined a group of six nurses at the entrance of the Naval Hospital. "The bus is coming," said an excited Martha as she spotted the white military bus coming around the corner. As they crossed the Bay Bridge into San Francisco, Nurse Jessica Knowles from Connecticut suggested that they go to the "Top of the Mark" hotel. "The restaurant and lounge provide great food and entertainment," she told the nurses who had just recently been assigned to the hospital. "It's a bit expensive, but we don't have many opportunities to spend our military pay. Plus the view from Nob Hill is absolutely stupendous."

As the sun was setting over the bay, six happy young women were on the bus heading back to the base.

A few weeks later Martha was called to Lieutenant Roberta Keller's office. "You are being transferred to the officers' section of the hospital. It's a smaller ward but it also serves the same types of patients as in this ward, men who have spinal and head injuries. One of the biggest challenges you will face in that ward is depression. These men who are ambitious and who anticipated luminous careers as civilians or in the military have been suddenly stunted. Your records show that you received high grades from your rotation as a student nurse at a mental hospital. You exhibited great composure and empathy. You were also not deterred from your ministrations to the patients by their outbursts and other abnormal behavior."

On Monday morning Martha Lepage made her acquaintance with the Naval and Marine officers on the ward under the direction of Chief Nurse, Lieutenant Commander Cynthia Walmsley. The ward contained twelve beds and there were eight private or quiet rooms. In one of the private rooms Nurse Walmsley introduced, "Lieutenant Junior Commander Mortimer Weigand we have just received a new nurse to assist us. Her name is Martha Lepage." Martha quickly noticed that the Lieutenant was unresponsive. Nurse Walmsley continued, "Her records which I just finished reading show that she comes from your hometown, New Bedford, Massachusetts." Martha observed just a slight peek coming from his eyes that quickly shut tight again.

Nurse Martha Lepage learned the reason for her sudden assignment to the officers' section of the hospital. Lieutenant Mortimer Weigand was being prepared to undergo a very delicate surgery to remove a piece of shrapnel that was lodged in his spinal column. It would occasionally press against the nerve and the pain was excruciating. Mortimer seemed to be coping with his pain by keeping his eyes firmly closed. The physicians were afraid that Mortimer's signs of depression would prevent a successful outcome and recovery from the surgery.

In about a week Martha's friendly and easy style had gotten Mortimer to look at her. And while she sat beside him while he ate his meals he would respond to her questions about the level of his pain, his years at the Naval Academy and he once volunteered a comment that his mother had moved from their home in New Bedford and now lived in the neighboring town of Fairhaven. Martha took this opening to speak of places familiar to both of them back home in New Bedford. Martha soon learned that Mortimer had spent most of his years away from the city. He had not attended any of the local schools. He knew of St. Luke's Hospital and some of stores in the downtown area and his neighborhood near the Wamsutta Club. They came from very different backgrounds. She sensed shyness in Mortimer. He indicated that his early childhood was sad but once his mother and father were divorced he started making friends and became quite good in sports and academics. He was extremely fond of his mother and of a young woman named Maureen. Since his graduation from the Naval Academy, a girl named Darlene with beautiful blue eyes had corresponded with him.

Martha encouraged him to write to her. Since his injury off the shores of Guadalcanal, letters from her had finally reached him in Oakland. He had not responded. He feared that Darlene would lose interest in him now that he was injured. A few weeks later Mortimer was beaming as he read a letter from Darlene that ended with "my love always."

This progress was related to the physicians who scheduled the surgery. The surgeons were optimistic that the operation would not only relieve the pain but also allow Mortimer to walk. Martha prepared Mortimer for the day of the surgery. Prior to going under anesthesia Mortimer had shared some very painful stories of his past with Martha. She felt blessed that he had been able to unburden himself.

Round Corners

Chapter Forty-eight

After Allied troops broke through the Atlantic Wall at Normandy, Lieutenant General Omar Bradley launched an offensive into France. After a slow start the offensive gathered momentum, and the German resistance collapsed as scattered remnants of broken units fought to escape to the Seine.

Late in July Robert and Larry and the Transportation Corps' Motor Transport Brigade were shipped to the coast of France. The Allies had observed a weakness in the German blitzkrieg or "lightning war" that used overwhelming forces of tanks, infantry artillery and air support moving at high speed to break through enemy lines. German forces quickly overran Belgium, the Netherlands and France without pausing to establish supply lines. The problem with racing beyond the supply lines was that the troops needed those supplies, particularly gasoline that powered the mechanized forces.

Robert and Larry were assigned a battered "Jimmy", the field operation nickname given to the new General Motors truck they had used in Texas. Larry questioned, "Robert, can you work your magic on this ugly piece of machinery?" While they awaited further orders, Robert and Larry took advantage of the supplies available in the motor pool maintenance shop. They replaced brake bands and broken shocks. For two days Robert worked under the hood, cleaning the carburetor, replacing spark plugs, even the head gasket, balancing the fly wheel until he was satisfied that their "Jimmy" was as tuned up as possible. Larry commented, "It doesn't purr like a cat but my test runs have been great."

In the bay of the maintenance shop, the two men from New England made their acquaintance with mostly black men. These men from the south were friendly and jovial. Martin Colley, a lanky black man working on his vehicle in the bay next to Robert, came over, "You seem to know what you're doing under that hood. Do you mind coming over? I can't seem to get the timing right."

The challenge for the Allies was to establish a supply line, and quickly, to support the plan to chase the Germans across northern France into Germany. The difficulty was compounded because the Allies had bombed the rail network to slow the German's supply effort that had once gone in the opposite direction. A strategy was developed that become known as the Red Ball Express. Truck companies that had amassed in Cherbourg off the coast started a convoy of carrying supplies on a 125-mile run to the forward logistics base at Chartres.

Designated two-lane, one-way roads were reserved for the truck convoys. The trucks were distinguished from others by a red circle or ball painted on the doors. The northern route was closed to all traffic except convoys delivering supplies, while the southern route was closed to all but returning trucks.

Larry and other drivers received the following instructions, "Maintain a 60-yard interval between vehicles. This will present less of a target to German bombers. Your top speed is not to exceed 25 miles per hour. Passing is not allowed. During night runs, use the "cat-eye" headlight covers."

When Larry came back to his Jimmy he saw Robert painting the Red Circle on the doors of the vehicle. "What's that?" asked Larry. Robert had also painted "Dolly" on the side panel. "Ah-yuh, I forgot. You're in love."

Before dawn the next morning Robert and Larry joined a convoy of seven trucks with a Jeep escort in front and back. The "Dolly" had been loaded with artillery munitions. Robert found himself praying,

"Please God we don't come under any air attack. With this load, we'll be scattered all over the countryside."

Traffic controlled points had been established that operated around the clock at principal intersections and in towns. The personnel who managed these control points regulated the convoys and other vehicles, civilian or military, that used the dedicated highway. They ensured that the Red Ball convoys had the right-of-way in all cases.

As the "Dolly" proceeded toward the front, Robert kept pointing out destruction that could be seen in the small villages nearby. After a while Larry interrupted, "Thanks for being a tour guide. However, I need to keep my focus on the road and the progress of the convoy." A little later Robert saw a disabled tank off the side of the road and fearfully realized that this was not a ride in the countryside.

One of the Jimmys became disabled and was quickly pulled off to the side of the road. The officer in the lead Jeep instructed the crew, "Stay with your vehicle. I'll alert the next maintenance vehicle we come across to come back to do repairs and get you on the road. Good luck."

The convoy arrived in Chartres by mid-afternoon. The city had suffered heavy damage from Allied bombing as they sought to soften the resistance of the Germans. With all the destruction around them, Robert and Larry were surprised to see the huge Cathedral of the city still intact. Before leaving on their return trip to Cherbourg the men of the convoy went to a bivouac rest area on the outskirts of the city for a hot meal. Upon inquiring about the incongruity of seeing the cathedral rising high above the landscape while the rest of the city was in shambles, a soldier assigned to the kitchen crew related, "The Cathedral had been ordered to be destroyed. A Colonel Griffith questioned that strategy and volunteered to go behind enemy lines to find out whether the German Army was occupying the cathedral and using it as an observation post. After his reconnaissance mission,

186

he reported that the cathedral was clear of enemy troops. We later liberated the area."

The Red Ball Express operated 24 hours a day. So after a brief rest on bunks in one of the barracks, the Dolly and its crew were off on another round trip to Chartres. While Larry slept, Robert was up about two hours earlier than departure time, so that he could examine his Jimmy. He changed a tire whose inside wall had developed a bubble from glancing off a sharp rock as they approached Cherbourg.

Each day the routine was the same. Sometime the cargo that they transported was less incendiary and both would sigh with relief. Increasingly, wounded soldiers became part of the cargo on the return trip. A Red Cross on a white banner was strapped over the open truck cargo area with the hope that the Messerschmitts of the Luftwaffe would not attack. Robert was given some quick training in first aid so that he could give some assistance to the wounded men. These men were dropped off at a staging area some miles from Cherbourg for a flight to England.

Round Corners

Chapter Forty-nine

As the weeks went by the convoys came under increasingly heavy fire. Strafing became a too common occurrence. On one trip Robert began to hear a steady buzz which he didn't manage to place immediately. "There they are!" exclaimed Larry pointing to his left. Bending down, Robert saw them too. "Nine...ten...eleven...twelve... there are twelve of them," cried out Robert. "What's that fellow up ta?" asked Larry to himself. The last plane in one leg of the V-shaped formation had broken away from the others. "It looks like its diving toward the ground," answered Robert. The rest happened so quickly that Robert didn't have time to be frightened. The plane doing the nose dive had disappeared from sight. "I think he crashed," stated Larry but Robert could still hear a menacing roar. It flew over the convoy, along its whole length, from front to back, so low that Robert and Larry instinctively ducked.

Then the plane disappeared and Robert wondered, "Is he gone?" A few minutes later they heard the rattle of a machine gun behind them. The plane had returned attacking the convoy from the rear. The "Dolly", that was toward the head of the convoy, disappeared under a heavily wooded area of the road. It escaped being hit. The lead Jeep just kept on going and the remaining convoy followed. As they made a wide turn in the road, Robert strained to see the end of the line. "It looks like we've lost a few trucks and I don't see the Jeep bringing up the rear."

Sometimes the trip was uneventful. On occasion they received a boost in morale as they passed a downed German fighter with the distinctive Balkenkreuz insignia on the fuselage. The Allies had started to position anti-aircraft artillery along this important supply route.

Through the months of September and October, the Dolly with Robert aboard and Larry at the wheel continued its daily circuitous route to Chartres and back. Every ten days the crew got a break for twenty-four hours. Robert spent most of that time working on his Dolly. It was getting more and more difficult to find the right parts. He often had to improvise.

At one of the bivouacs along the route from Chartres, Robert bumped into Martin Colley and each was introduced to their drivers. The division between black and white companies was beginning to be adhered to less strictly. A convoy was now made up of travel ready trucks and crews. The white crews welcomed this change since the great majority of those who operated the traffic controlled points (TCP) were black soldiers. It was the TCP troops that kept daily records of each convoy's arrival times, logged their destinations, and classes of supplies that each convoy truck carried. They also had maps that showed the location of refueling points and maintenance shops. On occasion they provided an alternate route for the convoy that was faced with some obstruction further ahead on the route.

During this time the Allies were reconstructing the French railroad system. The truck convoys were doing an excellent job of supplying the war efforts on the front lines. However, it required a large contingent of troops and a heavy supply of fuel that was always in great demand.

In early November, northern France received a heavy snowstorm. The eight to ten inches of snow was wet and heavy. The convoys on the Red Ball Highway just kept on rolling. Robert and Larry were part of the second convoy to head out of Cherbourg after the snowfall. Robert had made sure that his Dolly was equipped with a good set of chains for her tires. The trip was long and arduous as trucks slipped off the road. Robert would take the heavy chain fastened to the hooks on the front bumper to pull other trucks out of a ditch. Larry called out from the drivers widow, "Soldier, where's the shine on that chain?" He smiled thinking of how important it all seemed not so long before in Texas to have the chain sparkling. But now he had to use the skills he had first learned in the logging trails of Maine.

Larry could see Robert fastening the chain to the hooks on the front bumper of a truck whose left front tire was stuck in a ditch. The more the driver tried to straighten the front wheels and drive it out, the more it slipped into the ditch. Robert gave the all clear sign. Larry had his rear tires firmly in the middle of the road. While in reverse, Larry lifted the clutch slowly and felt the strain on the rear axle as the truck bucked under him. In slow motion Larry saw the hook that had been welded to the extremely rusted front bumper of the vehicle come flying off and whipped around hitting Robert on the right side of his head.

Larry quickly stopped his truck and jumped out of the cabin, running to Robert's side. Other men also came running to the scene. All could see that Robert had received a fatal blow. His head was smashed and bleeding profusely. He never regained consciousness and died in Larry's arms. For what seemed like hours to the other troops circling the scene, Larry just held on to Robert with tears streaming from his eyes and mixing with the blood all around the two of them. No one interrupted this sacred moment. Eventually, Larry asked for assistance in placing Robert on the flat bed of the Dolly. The leader in the front Jeep agreed that Dolly and two other trucks could break formation and travel to the next checkpoint only a few miles ahead. However, he insisted that the companion in his Jeep was to take the co-pilot position in the Dolly and keep an eye on Larry.

Round Corners

Book Nine

Round Corners

Book Nine

Chapter Fifty

Putting pieces together:

On a Friday morning after the surrender of Germany to the Allied forces, Detective Bill Normandin met with Homicide Chief Inspector Daniel O'Malley in his office. During the war years the case of the infant skeletal remains had been set aside. Although the circumstances of the discovery were strange, to date they had no proof that a homicide had occurred. Inspector O'Malley had decided to resurrect the case. Bill was expectantly hopeful that some of the studies that had been conducted by David Rubin a few years before would provide some enlightenment as to the discovery of the skeletal remains found in the Spooner residence.

Inspector O'Malley informed Bill, "I have invited the assistant coroner, Mr. Rubin, to join us this morning. He should be here shortly. I thought it would be very helpful to have him explain to us the quite technical findings of his report on the earth samples that he prepared for us over three years ago."

While they waited for David Rubin, Bill reminded the Inspector, "Our fingerprint people in the police department could not match Mortimer's fingerprints that we had received from the military with the fingerprints taken from the box that contained the skeletal remains."

Bill was still standing in front of the Inspector's desk. He started pacing to the window, looked out, scratched his head and returned to his former position in front of the desk. O'Malley observed these actions and thought to himself, "My young detective is considering other options."

Bill squinted and said, "Even if the prints on the box do not belong to Mortimer, it wouldn't necessarily exclude him from being the person behind this strange concealment of human remains. From what we know of his earlier mental state, especially the suspicion that he destroyed his own pet in an equally monstrous manner, I still feel that he has something to do with this strange event. He could have engaged someone to do this deed for him. We know from the contractor at the site that the construction of the box and its placement behind the wall of the upstairs bathroom required a degree of skilled workmanship."

Inspector O'Malley cautioned his young detective, "Remember, as detectives, our internal sense and suspicions can prove helpful but not if it obstructs us from observing other possibilities. Mortimer certainly can be characterized as a person of interest. We need to keep an open mind in our continuing investigation."

Bill nodded in agreement.

David Rubin knocked on the partially opened door of O'Malley office. "Come in, Mr. Rubin," welcomed the Inspector. O'Malley observed that David Rubin's dark ponytail that hung down below his shoulders seemed to have grown longer since they started working on this case some years earlier.

David was invited to a chair in front of O'Malley's desk. When he sat down, Bill Normandin also finally took a seat. Inspector O'Malley started, "We're reviewing the reports you prepared in the past. I've read them again carefully but I thought you could assist us in appreciating some of the more technical aspects of your findings."

O'Malley presented a copy of the report to Bill, "I had another copy typed out for you, Bill. You can follow along with us as Mr.

Rubin explains his findings and conclusions. Plus, feel free to ask any questions." As O'Malley said this last statement, he thought to himself, "I hardly needed to permit Bill that freedom. We would be hard pressed to find Bill to be a passive listener."

David Rubin started, "First, the very small sample of earth contained in the cranial part of the skeleton provided the usual elements found in the crust, or outermost layer, of our earth. Normally, only traces of calcium are found in the earth layer. The level of calcium found in that sample far exceeded the normal amount that was found in the samples taken from the Spooner property on County Street. However, we did find that the samples from Saratoga also contained elevated levels of calcium. That is in keeping with minerals found in drinking water and especially the spring waters found in that area of upstate New York."

Inspector O'Malley asked, "Were you able to identify a relationship with any of the springs adjacent to the Spooner property in Saratoga or the one at the racetrack?"

"That was my initial expectation," answered David. "The level of calcium at all three springs areas where we collected earth samples were different. Both the Polaris and Hathorn Springs adjacent to the Spooner property had levels of calcium closer to the level found in the skeletal remains. However, the level of calcium of the racetrack sample was minimal. It would be difficult to exclude this as a probable area since it is a large a piece of property which has been disturbed significantly over the years."

"Many analytic studies have been done of the composition of the waters of the springs in up-state New York and other parts of the country," continued David Rubin. "This information was available to me. The Polaris Spring, even though it is separated from the Spooner property by a marsh, contains levels of bicarbonate and sodium similar to the amounts found in the samples tested on the property and also found in the sample taken from the skeletal remains."

Bill interjected, "David, if I hear you correctly, the level of calcium and sodium found with the skeletal remains points to the probability that the infant's body was buried and decomposed in the ground that exist in the Saratoga area. Is that your finding?"

"My conclusion so far," answered David, "is that it excludes the probability that the decomposition occurred on the property on County Street and supports the theory that the infant was buried on the Spooner property in Saratoga."

Round Corners

Chapter Fifty-one

Inspector O'Malley asked, "Mr. Rubin, are you available to spend some additional time with us? I would like to review the information we have collected in reference to this case. I hesitate to call the discovery of these small human remains by the term "case" as it makes it so impersonal. You may be able to shed some light on the evidence that has been collected to date that will assist Bill and me to develop a plan for further investigations."

"To my knowledge there are no scheduled examinations this morning. I would like to call Dr. Kendall to make sure that no new developments have arisen since I left the lab last evening," answered David Rubin.

The Inspector pointed to the telephone on his desk as he invited Bill to join him in the hall providing David Rubin some privacy. Bill, knowing that his chief did not drink coffee at work said, "I'm going to get David and me a cup of coffee. Do you want anything?"

"I'll go with you and get some cold water," answered the Chief Inspector.

When they returned to the Inspector's office, David Rubin was waiting for them in the doorway.

Bill presented David a cup of coffee, "I thought you might want a cup. It has cream and two sugars."

David thanked Bill and said to the Inspector, "A patient died in the hospital last night and the family is still discussing the issue of an autopsy. Otherwise, the lab is quiet this morning. If an emergency comes up, he knows where to find me."

The Inspector sat at his desk with the two young men seated facing him. Bill pointed to the window, "The fog is finally starting to lift. We may see some sun today. It's been a few days now."

The Inspector started, "Let's first put together the facts of this case. First, the skeletal remains of an infant were found in the bathroom wall under renovation. Second, Mrs. Abigail Spooner and her son, Mortimer, vacated that property some years ago. Three other persons had been in residence just prior to moving away from the family home; Mrs. Moriarity who served as housekeeper and personal assistant to Mrs. Spooner, her daughter Maureen and Mr. Horace Bloom, the chauffeur and caretaker."

Bill continued, "Mrs. Spooner had married an Ethan Weigand from New York but they divorced when Mortimer was around five years old. The last I heard Mortimer was serving in the South Pacific. He should be in his late twenties by now."

The Inspector added, "As we all know Mrs. Spooner also owned a summer property in Saratoga Springs, in upstate New York. She purchased it after her divorce from Mr. Weigand. It was sold over four years ago. I've been informed by Mrs. Moriarity that her daughter is a little older than Mortimer. Maureen is married and lives in Maryland."

David made his contribution to the list of facts, "We know that it takes approximately two years to reach the state of decomposition observed in the skeletal remains of an infant. And that is for a body that is buried in the ground not just exposed to the elements of scavengers and weather. We have evidence in the cranium of the skeletal remains, that the body was first buried in the ground, removed, cleaned and then deposited behind the wall of the Spooner residence on County Street. Mr. Joao Pimentel estimated that the remains were placed in the wall two to three years before they started renovations of the house. My analysis of the plaster taken from the bathroom wall supports such a theory."

Bill jumped in, "That means that this infant was born and died when the Spooners still lived and owned the properties in New Bedford and Saratoga." Reluctantly Bill added, "Maureen, Mrs. Moriarity's daughter, was of childbearing age."

Inspector O'Malley cautioned, "That may be a fact but we need to be careful not to reach a conclusion that she is the mother of this child. However, it is this kind of information that can point us into a direction in this investigation."

David Rubin added to the thought process, "We have sufficient evidence that shows the body was not buried on the County Street property. There is supporting evidence that decomposition occurred in soil similar to that found on the Spooner's Saratoga Spring property."

The Inspector directed, "Bill, with this information in hand, I want you to pursue official records in the Saratoga Spring area of a birth between three and no more than six years ago. Search records in either the town or hospital files for a male or female child born to a Maureen. The last name could be Moriarity or the last name of the child's father, whose identity is unknown. Check the records in New Bedford as well."

David continued, "You have evidence that Mortimer's official military record of his fingerprints do not match those found on the box of remains. We need to collect the fingerprints of other members of the household."

O'Malley agreed, "This requires some delicacy. I have not spoken to Mrs. Spooner and Mrs. Moriarity since the story was carried in the newspapers about the discovery in the County Street residence. In my initial interview both women were extremely cooperative and showed no nervousness. Mrs. Spooner volunteered quite openly about her son's problems. She did emphasize that he had outgrown them, especially after the divorce from her husband. When I interviewed Mr. Bloom, the newspapers had already contained the story. His revelations about Mortimer still affected him. I'll review how we'll obtain these fingerprints with Police Chief Downey."

O'Malley saw Bill squinting and asked, "What's on your mind, Bill?"

Bill answered, "There is one person we tend to overlook who may not have been living in the County Street house at the time but would have been very familiar with it. That's Mr. Ethan Weigand."

Inspector O'Malley and David Rubin sat quietly turning over this thought in their minds. "You make a good point," stated the Inspector. David Rubin nodded in agreement.

Round Corners

Book Ten

Round Corners

Book Ten

Chapter Fifty-two

Coming home:

Grubby's prediction that he and Claude would soon be on their way home, turned out to be true and even sooner than expected. On New Caledonia the Seabees had accomplished their mission of building structures that had supported the South Pacific multiple military campaigns. After the surrender by Japan, large troop deployments were leaving the many islands and returning to the United States mainland.

New Caledonia which had served as a staging area for many of the conflicts, now served as a depot for returning troops awaiting ships to transport them back to the United States. That influx of troops at Noumea had kept Claude very busy in the bakery. Along with bread and rolls, the emphasis was on baking and decorating cakes. Decorations included a company or division's name and an attempt at drawing their insignia.

One evening Claude told Grubby, "One of our bakers has discovered that he has a real talent for drawing. He's thinking of taking up art, probably oil or water color painting, when he returns state side."

Grubby questioned Claude, "Frenchie, what do you think you'll do when you return home? Other than getting married to your sweetheart. Any thought of becoming a baker?"

Frenchie replied, "Anne wrote in one of her letters that a bakery in the city is going gang busters since it started baking, slicing and packaging a white bread under the brand name, Sunbeam Bread. It features a color illustration of Little Miss Sunbeam on the wrapper. Anne heard that a French Canadian family owns the bakery and it's located in the same section of town where we live. My older brother, Al delivers bread and pastries door to door and gets some of his product from that bakery. He's met the owner a few times. I'm sure to look up that job opportunity. It seems like a good fit. What about you, Grubby?"

Grubby pulled out his pack of Lucky Strikes that was rolled up in the left sleeve of his white t-shirt. "Want a smoke?" asked Grubby. Frenchie nodded. As they sat on the back stoop of the mess hall, puffing on their cigarettes, Grubby pondered, "I'm planning to get back to construction. My dad tells me that the unions are especially open to hiring returning G.I.s. My area of the building industry, of course, is the maintenance of vehicles and other machinery used in construction. The Teamsters Union that covers the New York City area is powerful and word is the Mafia has its hands all over it. A name like Ralph Papaleo wouldn't hurt."

A few months after the end of hostilities, the Noumea port was quieting down. When Grubby met Frenchie after lunch on a rainy day in December, 1945 he announced, "I just got orders that I will be shipping out on the next troop ship which is expected to stop by here next Tuesday." "Have you heard anything yourself?" asked Grubby,

"Nothing definite or in writing," answered Claude. "Our cooking and baking schedules are greatly reduced. Our chief has already closed down one kitchen. He expects word to come down soon. He says the typing pool at admin can't keep up with the orders."

The next morning Claude found Grubby working on a piece of machinery that was being made ready to be loaded onto a freighter in port. "I just got my orders, Grubby. It looks like we will be on the same troop ship out of here."

"Great," said Grubby with a broad smile on his face. "I wonder whether we will be picking up Tom Singleton and John Winters from the New Hebrides Island."

"That would be quite a stroke of luck," answered Claude.

"If they're smart, they should take a different ship home," said Grubby. "I can still remember how seasick you were on the entire trip out here."

"You had to bring that up," stated Claude with the color of green moving into his face.

Claude continued, "I'm to report at the Fargo Building in Boston. It seems I have to make up some points before I get discharged."

Round Corners

Chapter Fifty-three

Mrs. Paradis had just finished cleaning her kitchen of the supper dishes. The kitchen was located at the rear of the house. When she went to the dining room to tidy it up, she heard someone knocking at the front door. She was a bit surprised. On weekday evenings in this hard working community which mostly consisted of eleven hour shifts in the textile mills, few neighbors visited each other. She observed tall shadows behind the window in the front door covered by a laced curtain. She pushed it aside and saw two men standing there dressed in army uniforms. She suddenly felt lightheaded. Part of her wanted to return to the safety of her kitchen and to reassure herself that this was only a figment of her imagination.

During sleepless nights since her young son, Robert had departed for the war in Europe; such visions had brought fear and trembling as she lay quietly next to her hard working husband. Taking a deep breath, she unlocked and opened the door. "May I help you?" she asked.

"Is your husband at home?" one of the Army persons inquired.

"Yes," she answered, "he's in the yard at the rear of the house feeding his chickens and giving them fresh water."

"Would you mind asking him to come to see us?" the Army person continued. "We have some news about your son that we need to share with you."

Mrs. Paradis welcomed the two men inside the front parlor. "Please be seated and I'll get my husband."

Mrs. Paradis turned and retreated to the rear of the house, holding on to doorways and chairs as she almost staggered to the rear door off the kitchen. At the top of the stairs, she could see her husband William in the fenced in area behind the chicken coop.

"William," she shouted out in a voice that sounded like that of a stranger. William looked up and the movement of his head asked, "What do you want?"

"Will you please come into the house? There are two men here who wish to speak to us. They're from the Army," she added.

William immediately stopped what he was doing and reassuring himself that the light framed doorway into the fenced area of his chicken coop was securely fastened came quickly up the stairs.

They both looked into each other's eyes that communicated fears that both had previously kept deeply buried within themselves. William was dressed in a pair of bib overalls and as usual had only the left suspender of the overalls on his shoulder while the right one hung by his side.

Together they went to the front parlor. When they reached it, the two military men were still standing just inside the front entryway. Instinctively, William put his arm around his wife holding her close to him and she just fell in close to him letting him hold her from slipping to the floor in a heap. They hadn't held each other in such a fashion and in front of others since the early years of their marriage.

"My name is Sergeant Timothy Crawford and this is Corporal Paul Frazier," started the soldier to the right that William observed held an envelope in his hands. "You may wish to sit down," he advised. Mr. Paradis holding on to his wife indicated that they would remain standing.

"We are sorry to inform you that your son, Private First Class Robert Paradis, died two days ago while serving his country in France," announced the Sergeant. He paused allowing all in the room to absorb the impact of his words. Mrs. Paradis seemed to almost disappear in the strong embrace of her husband who stood tall with an almost blank stare in his eyes. A large tear came down his cheek which he wiped away with his free hand.

"Your son died in an accident while on a mission to the front lines near the city of Chartres in France," continued the Sergeant.

"I have a letter from Major Phillip Cross extending his sympathy and thanking you for the sacrifice that you and your family have made to assure that our country and its people are safe," said Sergeant Crawford as he came forward and handed the envelope to Mr. Paradis.

As they continued to stand there quietly, Corporal Frazier spoke, "Do you have family members?"

William Paradis answered, "We have a son and daughter who are married and live nearby."

"Would you want us to inform them of this news?" asked the Corporal.

William looked at his wife and answered, "No. Thank you. We'll share this news with them." Mrs. Paradis started to sob as she envisioned the sadness that her son Raphael and her daughter Janet would feel at the death of their brother.

Sergeant Crawford continued, "If we can be of any assistance, whatever it may be, just contact us. We have an office in Fall River that covers the area of Bristol County." He took a card from his inner pocket and presented it to Mr. Paradis.

Together the two Army men stood erect and saluted. Then they turned and exited.

For many minutes Mr. and Mrs. Paradis just stood there, holding on to each other. Finally, William spoke, "Mother, we need to call Raphael and Janet."

Mrs. Paradis suggested, "Can't we wait until tomorrow? It's already late and everyone has to be up early for work tomorrow." In saying this, deep inside her was a wish that all this would turn out to be a bad dream.

"No, mother," he answered. "We need to be strong for them. We need to share this with them and also be supported by them."

Mrs. Paradis reluctantly agreed.

Round Corners

Chapter Fifty-four

Louise was sitting on Al Lepage's lap while Charlotte sat on the floor in front of him. It was their favorite time of day – story-time. Charlotte had become aware that her father didn't read the words of the picture books that their mother had brought home from the library. As he looked at the pictures, he created his own stories and all of them were funny and had a happy ending. Plus he ended story-telling by singing them a few songs. One of their favorites was of the peddler, "I have peaches, I have apples, I have lettuce but I have no bananas today!" Each night's rendition the peddler had an ever changing variety of fruits and vegetables but he never had any bananas today. The girls would laugh and join in the last verse, singing with gusto.

Al looked up as the telephone rang. Janet, who was at the kitchen sink cleaning up the supper dishes, wiped her hands on her colorful apron and went to the phone on the small table in a corner of the dining area. It was the table where Al spent considerable time on Friday evenings making up his collection slips for Saturday. During weekdays Al delivered bread and pastries to his customers, many living in the three-deckers near the textile and other manufacturing mills that lined the river of New Bedford. Saturday was collection day.

Al noticed that a look of panic came across Janet's face. After a loud exclamation, "What?" Janet lowered her volume and went into one of the bedrooms. When she came from the bedroom, Al saw tears running down Janet's round cheeks. She retrieved a handkerchief from her apron and wiped her face and blew her nose. She indicated to Al by her index finger on her lips to say nothing. And then by a nod of her head, asked him to come to the kitchen.

Al asked Charlotte, "Would you read to your sister, while I go speak with your mother? You are beginning to recognize some of the words in this book. Soon you'll be reading them all by yourself."

Al put Louise on the floor near Charlotte and gave her the colorful picture book of "Twig." It was one of Charlotte's favorites. Their mother Janet had read it to them many times and she had fantasized of finding an elf that would also shrink them down to a size so that she, her sister and young brother Joseph already asleep in his crib, could join the fairies, at least for a while. Charlotte was pointing out the illustrations to her younger sister as Al joined Janet in the kitchen.

"What's wrong?" asked Al. Removing her hand that covered her mouth, Janet softly spoke, "My father just called. He told me that two service men in uniform had just informed them that Robert was killed in an accident in France." Janet moved deeper into the kitchen hoping to be away from the curious eyes of her Charlotte. Al wrapped his arms around her and held her tight.

"He asked if we might come over," she continued. "My Mom is taking the news very badly. She needs our support."

"I'll go right down and see if one of my sisters can stay with the girls," stated Al. Janet added, "I think it is best we not tell our girls anything tonight. Make sure you tell them that downstairs."

As Al and Janet drove up to her parent's home in the Sassaquin area of the city, her brother Raphael and his wife Mildred were getting out of their vehicle. They waited for Al and Janet to join them before entering the house. Mildred approached Janet and hugged her expressing sorrow and promising support for her and the family. "Raphael is stunned into silence," expressed Mildred. "You know he's not one to say much, but he's hardly said a word since his father broke the news to him and asked us to come over."

Janet knew her older brother well and the deep feelings hidden behind a quiet exterior. As she glanced over to him, she was happy to see that her simple and outgoing Al was engaging him in conversation. The two men had always gotten along well.

Janet went over to her brother and held him for a brief moment. Raphael wasn't the hugging kind but she sensed that even as he just stood there quite stiff that he welcomed her expression of comfort.

Mr. Paradis met them at the front door. Janet spotted her mother seated on the divan in the front parlor and went over to her. Kneeling before her, she said, "Mom, I'm so sorry. It's difficult to believe that our Robert who was always so full of energy is no longer with us. We'll treasure the memories we have of him."

Mrs. Paradis looked up and agreed, "Robert was certainly a special young man." Tears were quietly streaking down both their faces as Mrs. Paradis accepted the tight squeeze from her daughter as she sat next to her on the divan. Mildred came over and together all three squeezed in on the divan with Mrs. Paradis in the middle. They started reliving some of their memories of the young Robert.

Mr. Paradis was still in his bib overalls and stood across the room with his son Raphael and his son-in-law Al. "Thank you for coming so quickly," he said. "I need to share this hurt I feel inside me with you or I'll explode or crumble. And I can't afford to do this in front of your mother," he said as he glanced at her. Without realizing it, all three men were holding hands in a circle. Over the years Al had become extremely fond of his father-in-law. He was a self-taught man. He was an expert loom fixer at the Wamsutta Textile Mill. He was unassuming, loved his family and found joy in his vegetable garden and the raising of his chickens after long days of troubleshooting at the mill. Al started recalling some of his contacts with Robert and soon all three men were remembering young Robert and his many exploits.

After a while Janet announced, "We are going to make some tea and sit around the dining room table. Do you want to join us?" Raphael said that he would rather have a cup of coffee, Nescafe instant would do fine. Mr. Paradis and Al settled for cold glasses of water.

At the table, Mr. Paradis picked up the envelope from the breakfront that had been given to him by the Army Sergeant. He had placed it there earlier after reading it. He summarized the contents of the letter, "Robert died from a truck related accident while part of a convoy delivering supplies to the front lines in France. He died instantly and did not suffer, according to this letter from Major Phillip Cross. He will be buried in a French cemetery with his comrades. After a successful conclusion of the war, we can arrange to have his body transported back to us and buried locally, if we wish."

Mr. Paradis had difficulty in finishing his last few sentences. He passed the letter to his son, Raphael. Everyone around the table was extremely quiet. While sharing their memories of Robert the mood of sadness had lifted slightly as they recalled mostly humorous and action packed stories of young Robert. But now the deep void of separation came rushing back.

Mrs. Paradis broke the silence, "It's time you all go home now. You have been a real comfort to us tonight but we all have extremely early starts tomorrow morning. On Sunday bring your children over and we'll have a nice dinner together. You father still has some squash and potatoes in the garden."

William Paradis joined into the plan, "I will dress a couple of chickens. Mildred, maybe you can deep fry some chicken pieces that we men all love so much."

Al suggested, "I'll bring a quart of Dawson beer and some Nesbitt orange soda for the children." Raphael and Janet said they would plan together different desserts. Janet agreed with the tenor of the discussion, "Let's make this a celebration of Robert's life. Our children will be able to understand and appreciate that."

Round Corners

Chapter Fifty-five

Lieutenant J C Mortimer Spooner Weigand was slowly awakening from the drug induced sleep that kept him unaware of the pain associated with the three and half hour surgery he had undergone earlier that day. The surgeons had discovered that the shrapnel they removed from his spine had lodged in one of the bones of his lumbar vertebrae. As the doctors had suspected, the shrapnel had not entered nor cut the spinal cord from which emanated the sciatic nerves that radiated down Mortimer's legs. When Mortimer experienced excruciating pain, it was because the bone was pushing and squeezing the nerves in that area. The physicians anticipated, that with the removal of the shrapnel and the delicate reshaping of the lumbar vertebrae, pressure on the nerves would be gone. With therapy and hard work, Mortimer should be able to walk again.

Once when Mortimer opened his eyes, a young woman held his hand. He tried to focus his eyes but returned to a state of semi-consciousness. In his mind's eye, the young woman resembled Maureen from his happy days caring for horses at Saratoga and at another time he thought he saw the deep blue eyes of Darlene, the beautiful young woman he had met in New York with his friend, Richard and who had been present for his graduation from the naval academy. In this phase of semi-sleep, he experienced a deep peace and a sense of being loved. It contrasted with the constant sense of inadequacy and rejection that loomed ever in the shadows of his mind.

Eventually, he awakened and glanced about the recovery room. No one was present. His eyes began to focus and he began to remember where he was and the events that had brought him to the naval hospital. As he lay there immobile, he started to experience that something was missing. He was able to move himself slightly as he lay in his hospital bed. As he did so, he thought, "I shouldn't have done that. Here comes the pain." But Mortimer did not feel any shooting pain down his legs. That's what he missed, the sensation of pain.

A male nurse came into the room and observed that Mortimer had his eyes wide open. "You're coming back to us, Lieutenant. You've had quite a long sleep. How do you feel? Any pain?"

Mortimer tested the movement of his head and was able to indicate a negative. The nurse continued, "Right now you are still under a lot of anesthesia. As that wears off, we can give you some morphine that will bring some comfort. Don't be afraid to ask for it. You don't need to suffer with pain."

After adjusting the tube that was dripping a solution into Mortimer's vein of his left hand, the male nurse remembered, "One of the nurses wanted me to tell her when you awakened. I'll get the message to her. She was with you after you came out of surgery but she had to return to her work in another ward of the hospital." He took out a piece of paper from the pocket of his white medical jacket and said, "Her name is Martha Lepage."

Every time a nurse or doctor entered his room, Mortimer looked up in anticipation expecting to see Nurse Lepage. When one of the hospital corpsman offered to assist Mortimer in having some warm broth that had been brought to him on a tray, Mortimer estimated that it was dinner time. The sunlight coming in through the windows was starting to extend its shadows. The salty taste of the liquid had Mortimer licking his lips. Mortimer had still not found his voice. After a few spoonfuls of broth, the corpsman helped Mortimer to drink a few sips of cool water. Mortimer lay back exhausted. As the nurse was cleaning the area around his bed and removing the food tray, Mortimer tested his voice and said rather strongly, "Thank you. That was very good." The nurse smiled as he left the room.

As the sun was setting, Nurse Martha Lepage came bouncing into the room. She was all smiles and resisted the urge to hug and squeeze this young man lying in the bed. Instead she reached for his right hand touching it delicately and said, "Lieutenant, it is so good to see you awake and with a smile on your face." Martha had prayed that her assessment that Mortimer would pull through the surgery was correct. Her experience in mental health wards had shown her that depression was very complex and when least expected could overwhelm a patient.

Mortimer spoke slowly, "Nurse Lepage, thank you for being at my side and giving me the courage and will to undergo the surgery."

Martha just squeezed his hand more firmly and happy tears made her amber colored eyes sparkle like gold. "How do you feel?" she asked.

Mortimer answered, "I'm starting to feel some pain in my back area where the surgeons worked on my back, but I still haven't experienced any pain down my legs even when I move them slightly."

"I'm so happy for you," commented Martha. "Don't be afraid to ask for some morphine, especially during the early stages of recovery from the surgery. It will help, even if it does cause you to be a little woozy."

"I have to go now," continued Martha, "but I'll be back tomorrow. I just finished my shift and I need to bring some of my nursing uniforms to be cleaned. As you can see, it was a bit of a messy day in the wards. Sleep well. Happy dreams."

Round Corners

Chapter Fifty-six

Martha came skipping down the stairs from her second floor room of the women's barracks. She had already been out in the early hours of the morning. Under the watchful eye of the Marine Sergeant, she and about twenty other navy nurses who were off duty on Saturday had marched for about an hour. They would be part of the award ceremony to be held on the parade grounds. A heavy fog had rolled into the bay and the exertion had her perspiring heavily. She hoped that the exercise would help her lose a few pounds around her bottom. Even though she was on her feet all day, she was discovering that her body shape was following that of her mother and oldest sister. The pear shape was growing at the bottom.

After marching, she rushed off to pick up her two nurse uniforms that had been washed, starched and ironed. After a shower that she took in the common bathing facility at the end of the corridor, she dressed, dried and combed her short, auburn hair and pinned on her nursing cap. She glanced into the mirror as she added a light coloring on her lips. Her rosy cheeks were still flushed and she agreed with the image that looked back at her that she looked great and was ready for her day.

She joined other nurses who were leaving the barracks for breakfast in the dining hall. She had carefully planned every moment of her morning. She wanted to spend at least an hour visiting her patient, Mortimer. She would have to cross the entire base to the hospital section that cared for naval and marine officers. And then she would have to return to this side of the base, crossing the length of the parade grounds, in order to reach Ward B for enlisted men. After Mortimer's successful surgery, Martha had been reassigned to her former ward.

She had to do all this and be ready for her eleven o'clock shift. However, the custom in nursing meant that one arrived on site as early as a half hour ahead of time. There the nurses ending their shift filled in their replacement on the conditions of the patients, the new directions given by the doctors, special things to observe and record. It was a matter of pride among the nurses that the nurse that they relieved left on time at the end of their shift. After a long shift even the most dedicated nurses were ready for the break.

At breakfast Martha kept pulling out her watch attached to her uniform as she chatted with the others at the table. One commented, "It looks like you are anticipating a hot date." Martha answered, "I am. I'm going to visit Lieutenant Weigand who had successful surgery on his back. I stopped in last evening and he was alert and out of pain. I'm hoping he continues to improve."

One of the other nurses kidded, "Sounds to me that there is more than a professional interest between you and this young man." Martha blushed, "He can use some personal encouragement during his recovery." The nurses in her party all winked to each other. Martha hadn't told them of Mortimer's depression and the concerns of the doctors prior to surgery. She had been relieved when she saw Mortimer so animated after the surgery. However, from her experiences in the mental health wards she had seen the extreme mood swings that could come over a patient seemingly from no observable cause. She prayed that Mortimer would be spared.

When Martha entered the Lieutenant's room, he was lying comfortably in bed and beamed at her as she approached him. He couldn't wait to tell her, "They massaged my feet and legs this morning, and there was no pain!" "I'm so happy for you," stated Martha.

Mortimer continued, "The doctors want me to move carefully. The corpsman indicated that the surgeon's only concern is to make sure we don't open the incision on my back and that it needs to be kept clean in order to prevent any infection. They hope to get me to sit up in the chair in a few days."

Both simultaneously reached out to hold hands.

Mortimer continued, "Do you think you can get me some writing paper and envelopes? I want to share this good news with my mother. Since I arrived six weeks ago, I only wrote once and didn't really say anything except to tell my mother where I was. Plus I want to make contact with Maureen, Darlene and my good friend, Richard Cuthbert. I've asked assistance from the commanding officer in trying to locate Richard's present assignment. I've lost contact with him."

Martha had heard about all these people in the days prior to surgery. It was a good sign that the Lieutenant was ready to catch up with his family and friends. She answered, "I have tomorrow off this week. After the award and medal ceremony, I'll come over with some note paper and envelopes." Looking at her watch, she announced, "I have to be on my way again."

"I'll see you tomorrow," said Mortimer with a huge smile on his face. He reflected that the time with Martha always went by too quickly.

On a sunny Sunday afternoon a few weeks later, Martha was pushing Mortimer in a wheel chair heading to a sitting area overlooking the bluffs of San Francisco Bay. She assisted him as he stood from his chair and walked about twenty feet to a bench facing the bay. Mortimer was beaming as he slowly lowered himself to sit on the wooden bench. Martha joined him.

On their way to the viewing area, Mortimer had told Martha, "I received two letters yesterday, one from my mother and one from Darlene. Both were happy to hear that the surgery had been successful and that I was beginning to walk again. They want to know when they can expect to see me."

Martha responded, "That's great, Mortimer." Both had started to call each other by their first names, dropping off all titles. "From your records, I see that the medical staff is looking into moving you to another facility where you will continue your recovery and rehabilitation."

"One physician is looking into a hospital located in our home state in the city of Salem," added Mortimer. "He told me that first lieutenant, Josiah Spaulding, who recently completed his three years as a pilot in the Marine Corps has associated himself with the Salem hospital. From his war experience and the injuries he saw on the battlefields, he is trying to achieve an alternative to lengthy hospitalization and to focus on short-term care and rehabilitation. He knows from experience that before our injuries we military men were in great physical condition and were trained to face and overcome obstacles. The doctor thought that I would be a good candidate for such care and that I could assist them in developing their treatment plans."

"That's less than a two hour ride from New Bedford," said Martha. "Your mother and other friends would be able to visit with you while you continue your treatment. That's great! I hope that placement comes through."

"My only concern is that the witches of Salem might get me," joked Mortimer.

Round Corners

Chapter Fifty-seven

Claude Lepage and Ralph Papaleo arrived in sunny California at the Port of San Diego. To Claude's and Ralph's surprise, Claude had not gotten seasick on his travel back to the States. On their orders they still had ten days before they needed to report to their local Navy office. Frenchie was to report to Boston and Grubby to Brooklyn.

On the journey from the Pacific Island of New Caledonia, Claude had met a sailor who was reporting back to San Francisco. Claude and Eduardo Ruiz had made plans to travel together to the city in northern California. Claude wanted to visit his sister, Martha, who was a Navy nurse at the naval hospital in Oakland across the bay from San Francisco.

After a night on the town Claude bid farewell, "Grubby, you've been a great friend. We need to make plans to visit each other once we are discharged. I'll show you around New England and you can introduce me to the sights and sounds of New York." Grubby agreed. Keeping the promise he had made before leaving for the South Pacific, Grubby wore his Dress White uniform. He hadn't unpacked it while stationed on the island. "I hope it still fits," commented Grubby. "There are not many opportunities left to wear it. I'll surprise them at home as I walk up the street in my clean, fancy white uniform. That will shock my mother."

While on the bus to San Francisco, Eduardo explained, "When we first came from Mexico, my family worked in the vegetable fields of Bakersfield, north of Los Angeles. When I say my family worked, I mean everyone worked including my younger sister who was eleven at the time and my younger brother who was only nine.

It was backbreaking work but after a few years we were able to put together enough money to move up to San Francisco. My father found work as a janitor in one of the hospitals and my mother cleaned rooms in a hotel. My younger brother and sister were finally able to go to school and I took some evening classes in English and worked in the Beaulieu Vineyards in Napa Valley during the growing and harvesting seasons."

Claude's sister Martha had arranged to meet him at the Greyhound bus station at Potrero Hill. It was a great reunion. They hadn't seen each other in over two years. After bidding farewell to Eduardo, Martha pointed out some of the local highlights as they walked to Union Square where they found an empty park bench. They had so much to share. Martha caught Claude by surprise when she informed him, "My term of duty will be over in a few months. I've put in to be a nurse at the Veterans Home in Napa Valley. I met the commandant of the home, Colonel Holderman, who is a combat-hardened soldier of World War I and the recipient of the Congressional Medal of Honor. He runs a great ship and has invited me to join his staff. About fifteen years ago he had the foresight to construct a 500-bed hospital. The home is on a 900 acre parcel of land with many smaller residential buildings spread around the property. It's just beautiful. It's nestled in the verdant Wine Country of Napa Valley. If you had more time, I would love to bring you there to see it. Many of our California patients are being discharged to the home."

Claude just stared at his sister in amazement. His little sister was all grown up. "Will you have time after your discharge to come back home to visit the family?" asked Claude.

"The commandant has personally agreed to give me three weeks before I need to report to my duties at the hospital," answered Martha.

"Be sure to bring pictures of the place," stated Claude. "Everyone will be so curious."

After dropping this bombshell on Claude, Martha said, "Let's get something to eat." And she directed him to a little sidewalk dining area of one of the hotels adjacent to the Square. There she pointed out, "let's try the California White Seabass Nicoise pour Deux. Notice the French. I've been looking for an occasion to try this summer dish. They place the sea bass that is poached on a bed of lettuce which is surrounded by fresh tomatoes, slices of red onions, boiled red skinned potatoes and cooked green beans. The platter is garnished with quartered hard boiled eggs and black olives. Two nurses shared this meal a few weeks ago. I'm dying to try it. It looked so good."

Claude commented, "That's very different from the way we prepare and eat fish back home. I'm willing to try. I'm famished. I can assure you, we didn't cook like that on the island."

While sharing this delicious meal, Martha brought up the news of their brother-in-law Robert's recent accidental death during his tour of duty in Europe. Claude had not received word of Robert's death. His mail from home was somewhere in transit trying to find him.

Claude was shocked, "I was just thinking as I landed in San Diego, that we are so fortunate that the war has ended and all our family members are returning home safely. What happened?"

Martha answered, "From the best I can piece together from the letters I received from home, he was killed in a truck related accident while bringing supplies to the front lines. It was part of a last push to enter into Germany."

"Janet must be crushed," he exclaimed. "She was so close to her little brother. I still remember the time that Al and Janet took all three of us kids to the airfield in Fairhaven. We chased the plane down the runway and went scampering into the ravine when it returned and buzzed just over the ground of the airstrip. Robert was always so much fun."

Martha continued, "Robert is buried in France. Our families will be having a Catholic Mass and memorial service. I asked Janet if they might consider waiting until you and I return home. I haven't heard anything about that, yet."

Before long the sea bass platter was clean. Martha pointed out a dish on the dessert menu, "What about sharing the Crème Brulee with the caramel glaze? You'll notice the French flair to this meal."

Claude nodded, "It looks great. I don't believe I ever told you that I was always called Frenchie once I left home. A guy who served with me in the Pacific called me that once and it stuck. He comes from Brooklyn and is just a great guy and loads of fun."

Round Corners

Book Eleven

Round Corners

Book Eleven

Chapter Fifty-eight

Together again:

When Detective Bill Normandin met with Homicide Inspector Daniel O'Malley, he reported on his findings about the birth records possibly relating to the skeletal remains. He stated, "During the five years of my inquiry, there were twelve births to a Maureen. None of them had Moriarity as a last name. In the Saratoga files there were five births. Three of those births were recorded in both hospital files and town records. In New Bedford all seven births were recorded in both hospital records and at city hall."

Bill continued, "When I inquired about the discrepancy that only three of the five births were listed at the hospital in Saratoga, I was informed that there are mid-wives that assist in deliveries at home. One person told me that young unmarried women are often sent into seclusion from their homes to up-state New York during their pregnancy. The families are hoping to avoid bringing shame on the family. There's a very active adoption agency in Saratoga but all those records are sealed. It's a state law in New York."

"Of the five births to a Maureen in Saratoga," Bill added, "I was able to quickly eliminate three of them. Two of the mothers were in their thirties and one was barely a teenager. Of the other two, one gave birth at the hospital and one used the services of a mid-wife. Maureen who gave birth at the hospital stills resides at the address on the birth record with her husband and three children. I could not trace the other Maureen. The mid-wives tend to have their own code of secrecy. Locally, I was able to track down all the birth mothers with the name, Maureen. Some had moved away from New Bedford but neighbors or families provided with follow up information."

Bill concluded, "Although we don't have proof, there is still a probability that Maureen Moriarity gave birth to a child with the assistance of a mid-wife during a stay in Saratoga. And on the death of the child, it was buried on the Spooner property and later moved to the house in New Bedford. We don't have any direct proof of this scenario, but we can't disprove it."

O'Malley praised his detective, "Great job of investigation, Bill. And I appreciate your caution in not jumping to a conclusion. A door is still open in our investigation."

"In the past week," Inspector O'Malley continued, "I interviewed Mrs. Spooner and Maureen's mother at the residence in Fairhaven. Both were well aware of the discovery of the skeletal remains found at Mrs. Spooner former home on County Street. The newspapers had not revealed that the remains were those of an infant or its location in the house. Both appeared genuinely surprised by the story that had been in the papers. They were not as calm as in my first interview but the nature of our conversation had changed radically. It was understandable. Neither gave any hint about the size and location of these remains. I approached the issue with various questions and comments hoping to see whether they would reveal anything that was not related in the press. And they didn't."

O'Malley added, "My interview with Mr. Horace Bloom was not as reassuring. If there is anyone hiding anything in this case, it would be him. He may be only a very nervous and suspicious man by nature. He may even have something in his past that makes him uncomfortable with the police. The women readily agreed to have their fingerprints taken. However, Mr. Bloom only agreed to it reluctantly. He didn't seem satisfied that this was now a standard procedure. He wondered why this wasn't done a few years earlier in the case."

"Have you received any results from these fingerprints," asked Bill.

"Our fingerprint people," answered O'Malley, "didn't find a match for the two women to any of the fingerprints either outside or inside the box. They couldn't be as assertive about Mr. Bloom's fingerprints. There was a set of prints on the outside of the box that contained the skeletal remains that were overlaid by the more recent prints of both Joao Pimentel and the young Lepage boy who was helping him."

Round Corners

Chapter Fifty-nine

A few weeks after Claude had visited with his sister, Lieutenant Mortimer sent word to her to come see him as soon as she had any free time. That evening at a little after 7 p.m. and still in her white nursing uniform, she came rushing into his hospital room which he now shared with three other recovering officers.

All greeted her warmly; Martha had that effect on people. Her inner joy and easy manner warmed a room and brought out smiles from her patients even those who usually carried a frown on their face.

"What's so important?" asked Martha softly as she came closer to the chair where he was seated near his bed. Her expression was all curiosity.

"Martha," he started, "I'm being discharged to that hospital in Salem. I'm due to leave next week."

"That's so great!" answered Martha. "You've progressed so rapidly in your recovery. Plus you'll be close to home."

Mortimer grabbed her right hand in his and kissed it. When he looked up, sadness was evident in his eyes. "I'm really going to miss you, Martha," he stated. "You've been like a sister to me. I'll never forget the burden you helped lift from my shoulders the night before I went into surgery. You brought me hope and awakened a sense of life in me that I never knew existed."

When Mortimer released her hand, the men in the room all hooted, "Go to it, guy." They didn't know the very special relationship that existed between these two people before them.

Martha blushed, "Oh, come on fellas." And turning back to Mortimer said, "Thank you, Mortimer. But remember you also blessed me with your trust."

A few days later she was saying goodbye to Mortimer as he slowly walked up the stairs of the white transport van that would bring him to the airport. He was flying back to Boston with a layover in Chicago. A hospital corpsman was accompanying him.

Martha reminded him, "I'll be home in a little over a month. I'll find my way to Salem and visit with you. If you can get privileges to leave the hospital grounds, I'll try to arrange to have you visit my large and crazy family."

While in Salem and before Mortimer had a chance to visit with his mother, he received word from Mrs. Moriarity that his mother had a heart attack. She had responded to some medication but the prognosis was not promising. Mrs. Spooner hoped that he would visit with her at the hospital in New Bedford and Mr. Bloom had offered to pick him up. She was hoping that he was capable of making the trip.

Two days later Mr. Bloom picked up Lieutenant Mortimer at the Salem Hospital. He had shed his crutches and now used a combination crutch and cane apparatus that clamped around his forearm. He still had boot-like shoes that supported him from what the doctors called "foot fall." They hoped that strengthening therapy would help with time. While his leg muscles continued to strengthen with exercise, his feet had suffered from the effects of nerve damage.

Mr. Bloom announced, "We are stopping at the train station in Boston on our way to visit your mother. We are picking up Maureen and her son, Patrick. Your mother had always hoped to see Maureen and her little boy. Mrs. Moriarity suggested that this was a good time for them to visit."

Mortimer sat in the back seat stunned into silence. It was difficult to believe that the group from County Street and Saratoga would all be together again. And of course, there would be the addition of the young Patrick. It had been such a long time.

Mr. Bloom picked up Maureen and her son at the curb. Maureen joined Mortimer in the back seat and Patrick loved the idea of sitting in the front with the chauffeur. Mr. Bloom's present employer had been kind enough to offer the use of his Nash Ambassador 4-door sedan for the trip. Mortimer just kept on looking at Maureen as if she was a mirage. It had been almost ten years since they had seen each other.

Maureen told him, "My mother kept me informed of your time at the Naval Academy and then your assignment on the USS Little that shipped out to the South Pacific. We were all so worried when we heard of the sinking of the ship and how you were wounded. The last few months we have been relieved to know how well you were recovering from the surgery. I was thrilled to get your letter from California."

Patrick got up on his knees and looked back over the seat to his mother. He had the same coloring and wave to his hair as Maureen. He asked, "Is this the man you told me about that loved horses and worked in the stables with you when you were in New York?"

"Yes, Patrick," she answered. "This is Lieutenant Mortimer. My mother and I lived in his home when I was a child. We spent our summers in the country in up-state New York." She pointed to the driver and said, "Mr. Bloom would bring us to the racetrack and we spent our days taking care of the horses."

"We had a grand time," interjected Mortimer. "Your mother was very good with horses. She knew how to calm down the sometime nasty ones who just wanted to kick their stables to pieces." "You must be quite good with horses yourself," commented Mortimer.

234

"I have my own horse," announced Patrick. "He's a Palomino. His color is a light chestnut. I've named him Blondie. I'm learning to gallop when my mother is not around." He said this as he glanced at his mother who shook a finger at him. "My father knows. He told me I can only ride that fast when someone from the stables is with me."

"Oh, you are a handful," remarked Maureen with a smile.

They went directly to the hospital. Mrs. Spooner greeted her visitors warmly but weakly. She was assisted in sitting up in the bed by her faithful companion, Mrs. Moriarity. Once she made Mrs. Spooner comfortable, she picked up her grandson. "Paddy," she said, "you are all grown up." He squirmed from her embrace and found his way to sitting on the hospital bed. Mrs. Spooner reached and rubbed her fingers into his hair. Softly she said, "You're a fine boy, Patrick." Mr. Bloom quietly observed these people who had been his family. It was good to see new life.

Mrs. Spooner had asked Mrs. Moriarity to have her friend and banker, Mr. Willard, arrange for two rooms at the New Bedford Hotel. Before leaving Mrs. Moriarity asked Mrs. Spooner's permission to say a prayer together. Mrs. Spooner was a Quaker. After a brief prayer, Patrick crawled up to Mrs. Spooner and gave her a kiss. "Have a good night," he added.

Two days later Inspector O'Malley read the obituary of Mrs. Abigail Spooner in the morning newspaper. He decided to go to the wake at the Wilson Chapel that evening. It wasn't very often that he had allowed himself to get so close to the people associated with one of his cases.

There to his surprise he was introduced to Lieutenant Mortimer Weigand and Maureen Moriarity and her son Patrick. He was especially surprised to see that Maureen had come up for the funeral. Later he learned that Maureen and her son had arrived earlier knowing that Mrs. Spooner was seriously ill but not anticipating that Mrs. Spooner would die. She originally had reservations for them to take the train back to Baltimore that morning. They had changed those plans and would leave in a few days.

When Lieutenant Weigand stood at the receiving line in full uniform one could hardly notice that he had any disability until one looked at the black boots on his feet. It was in striking contrast with the spit and polish shoes one saw on men in the military. Lieutenant Mortimer was curious as to why the Inspector had come to the wake, and inquired, "Have you known my mother for a long time?"

O'Malley answered, "Close to five years and soon after she moved into the residence in Fairhaven." It was evident that his mother had not related to him the nature of their relationship. O'Malley wondered if Maureen was equally in the dark.

On the way home, he knew this was a unique but very sensitive opportunity to interview these two people.

Round Corners

Chapter Sixty

Lieutenant Junior Grade Martha Lepage was greeted at the train station in Providence by over twenty of her relatives and friends. A caravan of cars had driven from New Bedford to welcome her after her years of nursing duty on the West Coast. Her brother, Claude, who had returned from the South Pacific some two months before, had organized the reception group. It hadn't taken any persuasion especially when they learned that Martha would be home for only a few weeks prior to returning to work as a nurse in California.

Claude had arranged the reception committee so that their mother and father were in the front of the line. Martha was stunned to see the group but her focus was directed to her parents. She was so surprised and pleased to see that they had made the trip to Providence to welcome her. She ran up to them, wrapping her arms around both of them. "Oh, it's so good to see you," she exclaimed. And she kissed each of them on both cheeks, expressing sounds of joy and love.

She greeted each one individually. Smiles and tears mixed together in great profusion. To the side were her younger brothers and sister. She couldn't get over seeing how much each had grown in the years she had been away. Her young sister Mary Ellen fingered Martha's white naval uniform. "I only thought men who went to war wore uniforms like this," she said. "You look so pretty." Martha hugged her and told her sister, "There's a whole new world out there. And you'll be part of it. Knowing you, you'll make quite the splash."

Toward the rear she saw her brother Al. Eventually she reached Al and Janet and their three children. "I'm so sorry about Robert," she said to them as she held Janet tightly for a few quiet moments. Janet held Martha out in front of her and said, "We'll be fine, Martha.

We are much loved and Robert will always be with us in our hearts. Our stories and memories of him will keep him alive."

Martha picked up Al and Janet's son into her arms. "He's already four years old," said Janet as she sensed the question in Martha's eyes. Charlotte and Louise stood between their parents and were just staring at their aunt who was so precious to them. Janet had made pigtails with their hair. Louise exclaimed, "What do you think of our hairdos?" flashing and shaking her head. "You both look so beautiful. Are you teenagers yet?" Martha kidded them. Charlotte answered, "I will be vey soon." "That can't be possible," said Martha. "That means I'm getting old."

On the ride home Martha was in the car with her sister Claudia and her husband Paul who drove his brand new Chevrolet. She joined Claude and his girlfriend Anne in the back seat. She learned that Claude and Anne were already making plans to get married. In the meantime he was looking for a job. He had been promised a job as a baker at Sunbeam Bakery once there was an opening. In the meantime he was helping out at the Paradise luncheonette on the Avenue. "I start at three in the morning baking muffins and other baked goods. I'm finished by nine in the morning and have the rest of the day to myself. I've taken up fishing. Dad and I drive out to the country and fish in some of the ponds. One of these days I'm going to land the big one. There are some good size largemouth bass ready for the taking," informed Claude.

"What are you doing, Anne?" asked Martha. "I'm in my last year at Bridgewater State College. After high school my parents took their savings and encouraged me to study to be a teacher. This year I've been assigned to be an assistant in a classroom of an elementary school in Raynham. I just love it."

She learned that Paul's work at the Fort in the south end of the city had come to a quick end as the war was winding down. Right now he worked at his father's nightclub in Acushnet. With the return of local soldiers to the area, the Barn was doing very well. Martha knew from her letters with her sister Claudia that work at the Aerovox was booming. During the war years government contracts in the industrial cities and towns had brought steady revenue to these municipalities. The federal and state governments were also upgrading the electrical grids that crisscrossed the country. New technology allowed cities to reduce the multiple strands of electrical and telephone lines that resembled spider webs on the city streets. The Aerovox produced transformers and other transmitting equipment used in power lines.

Claude informed Martha, "Janet's family readily agreed with your request to wait until we were all home before having the memorial service for Robert. It's going to be next Saturday, a few days before you return to California."

Anne, who usually sat quietly and listened to conversations around her, surprised Martha by saying, "One of Robert's friends in the service came to visit his family about a month ago. He brought some of Robert's things he had found in the barracks. Janet and her parents were surprised to learn that he had made a commitment to the girl he had taken to the prom. He had a photograph of Robert near their truck with her name, Dolly, painted on the side. He had written behind the picture and looked like he was planning to mail it to her."

"Robert's military friend, Larry Crowther, is from Maine. He will be coming back for the memorial service," added Claude. "Dolly will also be present. She still seems to be in shock."

Round Corners

Chapter Sixty-one

The Paradis and Lepage families plus their many friends gathered in the small chapel in the far north end of the city. Al and Janet had been married there. Al said to his father as he helped him up the stairs of the chapel, "It's a little difficult to believe that it is almost ten years since Janet and I were married here." Mr. Lepage who normally kept his thoughts and feelings to himself surprised Al, saying, "Al, you found an excellent wife and companion in life. Janet reminds me so much of your mother. She is full of energy and seems to keep everyone happy and safe without much effort. They both have a special gift. We are blessed to have them at our sides."

The mood in the chapel was not exactly festive but not somber either. Everyone was talking to their neighbors in the pews. The normal silence associated with a Catholic Mass was not to be found. The smaller Paradis family and their many friends sat on the right side of the chapel facing the altar. Mr. and Mrs. Lepage went over to speak with Janet's mother and father prior to the service. They were already seated in the front row. Raphael and Mildred and their two daughters were seated with them. Al joined Janet and his two daughters and young son, Joseph in the pew behind them. Dolly and her parents were in the same row.

When a small bell rang announcing the entrance of the priest and altar boys into the sanctuary, Mr. and Mrs. Lepage scooted off to the front row on the left side of the chapel. The congregation finally quieted down. The older Monsignor who was now in residence at the main rectory further down the road and adjacent to the main church celebrated the memorial Mass. William Paradis had been a good friend of the Monsignor and had helped in the building of the chapel so that it could more easily serve this section of the city. It now included a sanatorium and a developing community of new cottages encircling Sassaquin Pond.

Monsigneur Wilfred Berube was an affable, gentle man. As a young priest he had been known as a stuffed shirt and easy to upset. He had expected perfection in the exercise of the Sacred Liturgy and struck fear in his altar boys, the women who cleaned and pressed the altar linens, and the choir director. However, over the many years serving this congregation of simple, hard-working and mostly not well educated people, he mellowed as he discovered and learned to appreciate their humanness as well as his own.

His pronunciation of Latin and French that were part of the prayers of the Mass was impeccable. Over the years his sermons included more English than French as his congregation gradually included other nationalities than French Canadians. Also the younger members of these families were quickly leaving their French heritage behind as they melted into the so-called pot of America.

After a brief sermon the Monsignor spoke of a recollection he had of Robert, "We all know how Robert loved to work on anything mechanical, especially automobiles. Because of the grease that was so often on his hands, I had early on instructed Robert that he had to wash his hands prior to putting on his white surplice. After some urging and reminders, this action had become routine."

The Monsignor continued and a smile spread over his face, "On one Maundy Thursday of Holy Week, Robert came rushing in at the last minute, put on his black soutane, looked over at me and went to wash his dirty hands before putting on his surplice. He was in the group of young men who had been selected to have one of their feet washed. When I knelt before him with the basin of water and towel, he had removed his shoe of his right foot but had not removed his sock. I looked up at him and indicated that he needed to take off his sock. He bent over and reluctantly took off the sock and I saw a foot that was black, covered in dried mud. I wasn't sure if whether I should place it into the basin of water. But I reflected that the washing of feet in the time of Jesus was not just a liturgical act but a real ritual of cleansing."

The people in the pews smiled, looked at each other and exchanged brief words acknowledging this side of Robert. Mrs. Paradis looked a bit embarrassed but smiled at this recollection. Robert had explained to her that he had been at the edge of the pond catching tadpoles when he remembered that he had to get to church. "Un fils tres precieux," she had thought.

Prior to the Monsignor's blessing at the end of Mass, Robert's army buddy from Maine, Larry Crowther, stood in front of the communion rail dressed in his military uniform. He held the folded American flag in his arms close to his chest. He was remembering holding Robert as his life slipped away on the dirty snow-covered street outside of Chartres. In his Maine accent, he presented the flag to Mrs. Paradis, "On behaf of our Commander-in-Chief, I hav the honor of presenting you and your family our American flag. Robert served his country with honor. I had the privilege of riding with him to the front lines and back dozens of times. He was a comrade and best friend."

Tears started to flow quite freely in the congregation.

Janet had arranged with the Monsignor to play a musical piece on her violin just prior to the end of the liturgy. She wanted to express her grief at losing her brother and also to profess her hope that his brief, young life continued to bless them. She searched her music sheets that she had used while attending violin classes prior to her marriage to Al. When they were first married she would take out her instrument and play on occasion, usually when she was alone in the third floor tenement apartment. Now with three children her instrument had not been tuned or played for many years. She selected to play a brief section of Johann Sebastian Bach's Oratorio for the feast of the Ascension. When Al and the children were asleep she would go to the front parlor, close the door behind her, and retrieved her violin case that was lying behind the couch.

Janet had selected to play movement 2 of the Oratorio. The entire Oratorio had a total of eleven movements and normally took over a half hour to play. The movement entitled Evangelista included a recitation of the Evangelist Luke. She practiced playing each evening as softly as she could so as not to awaken her family or the neighbors whose house was only a few feet away. It surprised her that the dexterity of her fingers that had washed many diapers and cooked many meals, remembered the movements along the strings. Her bow needed successive applications of resin before it moved rhythmically over the strings of her violin.

Janet moved out of the pew with her violin in hand. Martha, who had arrived from California only a week earlier joined her in front of the communion rail facing the congregation. Janet had asked Martha if she was willing to read the selection from Luke's gospel that accompanied this piece. Martha readily agreed. She was a very composed and self-confident young woman. They had practiced together a few times, so that Martha would be able to recite the gospel reading to the flow of the music.

Janet played softly and Martha started reading:

"And he led them out as far as to Bethany,
and he lifted up his hands, and blessed them.

And it came to pass, while he blessed them,
he was parted from them, and carried up into heaven."

Silence and weeping filled the chapel. The Monsignor allowed the people time to embrace this sacred moment. He finally blessed the congregation, "Au nom du Pere, et du Fils, et du Saint Esprit."

Round Corners

Chapter Sixty-two

Chief Inspector Daniel O'Malley stood somewhat removed from the small group that was in attendance for the burial services at the Spooner family plot in the Mattapoisett cemetery. Mrs. Moriarity, her daughter Maureen and grandson Patrick stood on one side of the gravesite. Mr. Horace Bloom stood behind them. Mortimer and a young woman that the Inspector did not recognize stood on the other side. A clergyman, dressed in a colorful garb similar to a professor in a gown used at a graduation, was offering a reading which O'Malley did not recognize as a familiar text from the Scriptures.

The clergyman stood next to the family tombstone and three women stood across from him at the other end of the casket. O'Malley thought he recognized one of the women from his visits to Mrs. Abigail Spooner's residence in Fairhaven. After the reading and a few words, the clergyman approached Mortimer Spooner Weigand and extended a hand of condolence. O'Malley saw Mortimer introducing the young lady beside him to the clergyman.

Mrs. Moriarity knelt on the ground and kissed the simple, well-polished wooden coffin. Maureen assisted her mother to stand with young Patrick offering his hand to steady her. Mrs. Moriarity looked down lovingly on her grandson. Mortimer took a handful of dirt from the spade presented to him by one of the two cemetery workers who had approached after the brief service. He approached the coffin and sprinkled the earth lightly over it. It was more like a caress than the consigning of his mother to her grave. Mr. Bloom remained in his spot holding his chauffeur cap in his hands.

Mortimer, walking with an evident limp, approached the women who remained standing at the end of the coffin. He expressed his gratitude for the care they had bestowed on his mother. When the women moved away, Mortimer and the former household members comforted each other with embraces, holding hands and sharing words of encouragement. O'Malley observed the young lady who had been at Mortimer's side retreat from the gathering and was met by a young man who accompanied her as they left the cemetery grounds to a waiting vehicle.

Maureen broke away from the family grouping and approached Inspector O'Malley. He had hoped to speak with her before her return to Maryland. Unexpectedly, the young woman had taken the initiative.

"Inspector," she started, "I suspect that you'd like to speak with me." O'Malley nodded, "It may seem rude to do so on such an occasion, but I knew of your plans to return home."

"No need to apologize," added Maureen. "My mother spoke with me last evening of your investigation. I agreed with her that speaking with you prior to my departure would shed light. If you would provide me a ride back to the New Bedford Hotel, where Mr. Bloom will be taking my mother, Patrick and Mortimer for a light lunch I would be willing to speak with you along the way."

O'Malley readily agreed. Maureen, turning to her mother who was watching her with the Inspector, waved them on. The group followed Mr. Bloom to the Nash Ambassador parked in a small roadway of the cemetery.

The Inspector opened the passenger door of the front seat of the unmarked police vehicle. Maureen had agreed that it would make it easier to speak together than if she took a place in the rear of the vehicle. O'Malley drove off and both were quiet for a few minutes. "I'm extremely grateful that you have taken the initiative to meet with me," observed O'Malley.

Maureen spoke slowly, "This has been hidden too long. I'm anxious yet ready to unburden myself and others of this secret. When I was close to twenty I became friendly with a young man who worked for one of the horse owners who had brought three horses from his stable in Tennessee to compete in the Travers stake at the Saratoga Racetrack." Maureen took a deep, cleansing breath and continued, "After my young man returned to Tennessee, I discovered that I was pregnant. After keeping it to myself for a while, I finally informed my mother. We were beginning to make preparations to return to New Bedford usually two or three weeks after the closing of the race schedule in late August. My mother spoke with Mrs. Spooner and it was decided that I should remain in seclusion at the Saratoga summer residence during my pregnancy. Mr. Bloom would stay with me and see that all my needs were met, that is once he had delivered my mother and Mrs. Spooner back to the main home in New Bedford. Mr. Bloom would assist Mrs. Spooner to get a chauffeur and he would return and stay with me. Before leaving upstate New York, Mrs. Spooner had arranged to have a nurse/mid-wife assist me in my pregnancy and delivery."

O'Malley continued to listen and commented, "You were a very brave young woman."

"Truly, I was afraid and confused," Maureen responded. "This was my first winter away from New Bedford and the comfort and strength of my mother. The time of my pregnancy now seems to have gone by quickly. My health was good and I was active up to the last month. I delivered a little baby girl about three weeks prematurely. Colleen was beautiful. The plan was that I was to give her up for adoption. The premature delivery of Colleen delayed those plans. I attempted to nurse Colleen but it was difficult for both of us. Colleen wasn't thriving. My mother suggested that the mid-wife find and engage a wet nurse to feed my daughter. She found a young mother who had just given birth to a son. Her name was Grace. Colleen sucked hungrily from Grace's breasts and color came into her cheeks, but just as suddenly Colleen rejected being fed." Tears were now flowing down Maureen's cheeks. O'Malley offered the fresh handkerchief that his wife put into the breast pocket of his suit each day.

Maureen dried her eyes and cheeks and looking over to the Inspector for approval, blew her nose into the handkerchief. "Thank you, Inspector. I should have come better prepared." "You are doing just fine," O'Malley answered.

"Colleen became weaker and it seemed her light blue eyes looked at me for help," continued Maureen. "It broke my heart. Just five weeks after her birth, Colleen fell asleep peacefully in my arms and never awakened. The mid-wife fetched the doctor. It was too late. The doctor ventured an opinion based on our description of her condition that Colleen suffered from some obstruction in her digestive system."

"It was early spring when she died," said Maureen. "It was decided that we bury Colleen in the back yard. Mr. Bloom and I prepared a beautiful spot close to a small apple tree that would soon be blossoming. In the middle of June Mrs. Spooner and my mother joined us in Saratoga. Each day that summer we all laid fresh flowers on Colleen's grave. That summer I returned to caring for horses at the track. There I met my present husband Bob who was then an assistant trainer. When he returned to Maryland after the race season, I was heartbroken. We corresponded regularly by mail and occasionally he would call me. He missed me also. Between Thanksgiving and Christmas Bob drove up from Maryland and we were married by a Justice of the Peace. Together we drove back."

"The following year my mother informed me of Mrs. Spooner growing ill-health, so it came as no surprise that Mrs. Spooner closed the house in upstate New York and eventually sold it. About a year later Mrs. Spooner also sold her home on County Street to a relative and moved into the Fairhaven Residence with my mother as her companion," continued Maureen. "Last night my mother told me that little Colleen had been moved to New Bedford. It took me completely by surprise. In my heart and mind, I had continued to see Colleen lying peacefully under the apple tree."

"My mother informed me," said Maureen, "that she had always been perplexed as to why Mrs. Spooner had chosen to have my Colleen placed behind the walls of her bathroom. However, she did tell me that she and Mr. Bloom had been sworn to secrecy. Now that Mrs. Spooner has died, the reason for her choice will probably remain a mystery."

Round Corners

More to be

revealed

Clement R Beaulieu is a semi-retired income tax preparer. In the off-season he recently wrote and published his first historical mystery novel entitled, *Bad Lucky Number*, set in the mill city of New Bedford, MA. circa 1930. He lives with his wife Jo-Ann in the quaint neighboring town of Fairhaven. They have two adult daughters, Sarah and Julia, who live nearby.